Alexander Thom and Co.

The Thirtieth Report Of The Deputy Keeper Of The Public Records

And Keeper Of State Papers In Irland

Alexander Thom and Co.

The Thirtieth Report Of The Deputy Keeper Of The Public Records And Keeper Of State Papers In Irland

ISBN/EAN: 9783742805966

Manufactured in Europe, USA, Canada, Australia, Japa

Cover: Foto ©Andreas Hilbeck / pixelio.de

Manufactured and distributed by brebook publishing software
(www.brebook.com)

Alexander Thom and Co.

The Thirtieth Report Of The Deputy Keeper Of The Public Records

And Keeper Of State Papers In Irland

30 & 31 VICTORIA, CAP. 70, S. 24.

THE
THIRTIETH REPORT

OF THE

DEPUTY KEEPER

OF THE

PUBLIC RECORDS AND KEEPER

OF THE

STATE PAPERS IN IRELAND.

[14TH MAY, 1898.]

Presented to Parliament by Command of Her Majesty.

DUBLIN:
PRINTED FOR HER MAJESTY'S STATIONERY OFFICE,
BY ALEXANDER THOM & CO. (LIMITED).

And to be purchased, either directly or through any Bookseller, from
HODGES, FIGGIS and Co. (Limited), 104, Grafton-street, Dublin, or
EYRE and SPOTTISWOODE, East Harding-street, Fleet-street, E.C., and
32, Abingdon-street, Westminster, S.W.; or
JOHN MENZIES & Co., 12, Hanover-street, Edinburgh, and
90, West Nile-street, Glasgow.

1898.

[C.—9080.]   Price 8½d.

CONTENTS.

No. 12794.

Sir,

I have to acknowledge the receipt of your letter of the
27th instant, forwarding, for submission to His Excellency the
Lord Lieutenant, the Thirtieth Report of the Deputy Keeper of
the State Papers in Ireland.

I am, Sir,

Your obedient Servant,

(Signed)   D. HARREL.

The Deputy Keeper,
Public Record Office,
Four Courts.

30 & 31 VICTORIA, CAP. 70, SEC. 24.

THE THIRTIETH REPORT

OF THE

DEPUTY KEEPER OF THE PUBLIC RECORDS
AND KEEPER OF THE STATE PAPERS
IN IRELAND

TO THE RIGHT HONORABLE THE EARL
CADOGAN, K.G.,

LORD LIEUTENANT-GENERAL AND GENERAL GOVERNOR OF IRELAND.

MAY IT PLEASE YOUR EXCELLENCY.

1. In the introductory note to the Index to the Act or Grant Books, and to the original wills of the diocese of Dublin, 1272–1800, published as an Appendix to my 26th Report, it was pointed out that there were gaps in the sequence of Marriage Licences from 1572 to 1607, and from 1713 to 1741, which had occurred since the return was made in 1811 to the late Record Commission; and it was explained that the Index to the Marriage Index in the possession of H. Farnham Burke, esq., Somerset Herald, and was printed as Addenda to that Appendix. Since then most of the missing volumes have been found by Mr. Samuels, the Registrar of the Diocese of Dublin, amongst the Rule-books in his office. These volumes cover the periods 1572–1685, and 1718 to 1741, leaving those for 1685 to 1697 still wanting. The transcript has been found to have been, originally, so carelessly made, that it will be necessary to print a list of errata, which it is hoped will be completed in time for next year's report. A schedule of the four recovered volumes will be found at paragraph 74.

2. Mr. R. C. Maxwell, of this office, having again passed the examination for the Higher Grade in the Civil Service has been appointed to the English Local Government Department, and Mr. Jarred has been transferred to the same department. Mr. Charles Evelyn Royds, B.A., of Cambridge, and Mr. Charles J. T.

D. Grylls, B.A., of the same university, have been appointed to the vacant places on the 21st April and 20th October, 1897, respectively.

3. It appearing from the catalogue of the late Sir Thomas Phillipps' library that certain MS. books and papers in the nature of State Papers and Records, that had at one time been in the possession of State Departments in Ireland, were to be sold by auction at Messrs Sotheby's, application was made to the Lords Commissioners of Her Majesty's Treasury, through the Chief Secretary for Ireland, to have same purchased. This application was very cordially entertained both by Mr. Balfour and their Lordships, and Mr. James Mills of this department was sent over to examine them in conjunction with Mr. Warner, of the British Museum, and in the result twenty lots were purchased and transferred here. A schedule of them will be found at paragraph 72, and a Report, by Mr. H. F. Berry, on their nature and contents in Appendix I.

4. The Rev. H. C. Groves, D.D., a son of the Mr. Groves, one of the Sub-Commissioners employed upon the Chancery Records, by the late Record Commission of Ireland, has deposited some original records, which he found amongst his father's papers. They have been interpolated in their respective series, and a list of them will be found at paragraph 73.

State Paper Office

5. The papers of the Chief Secretary's Office for the year 1887 were received in March. They have been examined, checked and put up in 50 carton boxes numbered 3,300 to 3,358. The Index and Register of the same office for 1885, three large volumes, were also received.

6. From the Privy Council Office there came in April the papers of that Department for 1884 to 1888, contained in 55 cartons. These have also been checked and put up. The following books of the Council Office were received:—3 Letter Books, 1879-88, 8 Minute Books, 1839-86, 11 Order Books, 1876-86.

7. The searches made for the Chief Secretary's Office numbered 262, 49 more than in the previous year. Mr. C. L. Falkiner, Mr. J. H. Scaife of the Quit Rent Office, and Mr. J. H. Reddan of the Foreign Office, having respectively obtained permission of the Chief Secretary, have been permitted to make searches or examine State Papers.

8. As mentioned in last report the papers remaining in the Tower of earlier date than 1760 had been arranged in Chronological order, and placed in 13 carton boxes. To these papers a manuscript calendar was prepared in 1897, extending to 318 pages. The papers and calendar have been transferred to the Public Record Office.

9. The arrangement of the papers of the next period, 1760-99, has been commenced, and some progress made. A calendar of these has been taken in hand. Following the lines of the partial arrangement already existing, it is intended to treat these papers

in two classes: 1, Official Letters; 2, Miscellaneous Letters and Papers.

10. An important but unfortunately very defective series of books called " Private Official Letter Books," has been examined, and as far as the year 1769 transferred to the Record Office. The earlier books of this series contain chiefly entries of letters from the Lords' Justices to the Lord Lieutenant when in England. They thus tend to complete the historical value of the letters in the series " British Departmental Correspondence " already transferred. Two of the volumes consist of original letters from the Earl of Bristol when Lord Lieutenant, 1700-7. The later volumes are entry books of letters from the Irish Government to English Departments.

11. All papers connected with proceedings in Council for Unions or divisions of Parishes and changes of site of Parish Churches, down to 1845, have been collected, arranged according to Dioceses, and made up in thirty parcels. An Index-catalogue has been made; and they have been transferred to the Public Record Office.

12. A considerable quantity of papers relating to military affairs have been found, which complete or supplement series already transferred to the Record Office. They include letters from the Commander of the Forces (1804-29), the Home Office, War Office, London, Quarter-Master-General, &c.; also Militia Regimental Papers, Militia Depot papers, &c. These have been examined, arranged, parcelled, and with a few books of the Military Department, transferred to the Public Record Office.

13. Thirty-six volumes and a few parcels of papers of the Yeomanry Department were also examined, cleansed, arranged, and transferred.

14. Among the duties of the Yeomanry Department of the Chief Secretary's Office was the granting of licences for the sale of Gunpowder, and for the sale and repair of Arms. The applications, certificates and returns connected with these licences were very numerous. They have been arranged, cleansed, flattened, and made up in 340 brown paper parcels, in the following series: Gunpowder licences 1824-37 (with some earlier) arranged by counties; second series 1841-2 arranged chronologically; Arms licences 1822-37; return of Arms sold 1822-38. They have been transferred to the Public Record Office.

15. A number of papers relating to distress, famine and fever in Ireland in 1822 have been examined. They include applications for relief from different parts of the country, and reports upon them. These have been arranged by counties. Other papers relate to the general organisation of the relief; London and other relief committees; relief works; purchase and distribution of potatoes and meal; fever reports and medical aid. These have been arranged according to subjects. They have been transferred to the Public Record Office.

16. The papers connected with the Cholera outbreak 1832-4 have been put in order. The original arrangement had been under letters, according to the initial letter of the parish or dis-

trict from which the reports were received. This arrangement, admitting of ready local reference, has been carried out. The papers have been made up in 49 parcels and transferred to the Public Record Office.

17. In 1833 a Commission was issued to enquire into the condition of the Irish Poor. Sub-Commissioners went through the country and held local or parochial public enquiries in many parts of the country. For the purpose of these enquiries a very long series of printed questions was supplied to the Sub-Commissioners. At these enquiries all classes were usually represented—landlords, clergy of different denominations, farmers and other employers, labourers, and sometimes even professed beggars. A number of reports of these local enquiries have been found, containing replies to the questions, frequently in the words of the persons present. The answers appear generally to have been given with much freedom. The reports forthcoming have been arranged by counties; those best represented are Westmeath, Wexford, and Londonderry.

18. In the following year the Commissioners directed their attention to the condition of agriculture and agricultural holdings in Ireland. Similar enquiries were held by baronies. The reports preserved have been arranged according to provinces.

19. Beside those direct public enquiries, the Commissioners sought information as to the condition of those Irish who had settled in the manufacturing towns of England and Scotland. With this purpose they sent sheets of printed queries to the Roman Catholic priests of towns or districts where Irish were known to have settled. In several cases replies, sometimes of considerable interest, were received. These papers have all been transferred to the Public Record Office.

20. A considerable number of reports and papers relating to Distress in 1846-7 have been arranged by counties and made up in brown-paper parcels. Some of these need further classification, and will require to be inserted in the regular papers of their year.

21. A large number of papers relating to convicts and prisoners have been examined and arranged in three series:—

i. The series of Judges' reports on cases, with memorials, &c., in favour of the prisoners, has been completed to 1827, by replacing several files and parcels misplaced in other collections. The insertion of references to the added papers in the index has been commenced.

ii. Prisoners' petitions and cases not referred to judges have been arranged in years from 1798 to 1835 in readiness for indexing. They form 26 parcels.

iii. Papers relating to transportation or disposal of convicts have been arranged in years 1788 to 1835, in 15 parcels.

22. A transfer of Records to the Public Record Office under warrant was, as usual, carried out in December. The papers transferred have been incidentally noted above; a schedule will be found at paragraph 44.

TRANSFERS.

There have been transferred to and deposited in the Public Record Office during the past year the following records:—

22. From the Record and Writ Office, Chancery:—

Records.	Date.	Vols.	Prts.
Affidavits, ...	1878	44	—
„ Index to, ...	„	1	—
Answers, ...	1875-6	2	—
Appearances, ...	„	2	—
Attorneys' Licences, Register of, . . .	1863-74	9	—
Awards, Drainage, ...	1876	—	1
„ Piers and Harbours, ...	„	—	1
Bill Book, ...	„	1	—
Bills, ...	1875-6	4	—
„ and Answers, Index to, . . .	1876	1	—
Certificates, Chief Clerk's, . . .	„	6	—
„ Lower Scale, . . .	„	2	—
Commons, ...	„	1	—
Crown Land, Conveyances of, . . .	„	—	1
Depositions and Evidences, . . .	„	1	—
Dismantling Dead Rolls, . . .	„	2	—
Interrogatories, ...	„	1	—
Maps, Drainage, ...	„	—	1
Masters' Rota Book, ...	1867-73	1	—
Miscellaneous Documents, Index to, . .	1871-4	1	—
Motion Book (Rolls), ...	1875-6	2	—
Motions, Notices of, . .	1876	1	—
„ Landed Estates Court, . . .	„	5	—
Notices, „	„	6	—
Orders, English (11 & 12 Vic., c. 46), . .	1870-6	9	—
„ Lord Chancellor's Chamber, . .	1876	3	—
„ „ Court and Chamber, . .	„	3	—
„ Rolls' Chamber, ...	„	1	—
„ „ Court and Chamber, . .	„	9	—
„ Vice-Chancellor's Chamber, . .	„	1	—
„ „ Court and Chamber, .	„	2	—
„ General Index to, ...	„	1	—
„ and Notices of Motions and Miscellaneous,	„	5	—
„ „ „ (I. R. O.), Register of Service of, .	1875-6	1	—
Patent Roll, ...	1876	—	1
„ „ Calendar, ...	1850-73	1	—

RECORD AND WRIT OFFICE, CHANCERY—*continued.*

Records.	Date.	Vols.	Pris.
Petitions, ...	1875	8	—
„ Index to, ...	„	1	—
„ of Appeal and Answers thereto, ...	„	1	—
Receivers' Accounts, ...	„	6	—
Recognizance Roll, ...	„	—	1
Recognizances, ...	„	—	1
„ „ Orders to Vacate, ...	„	—	1
Rule Books (Side Bar Order Books), ...	„	6	—
Summonses, ...	„	6	—
„ Originating Administrations, . . .	„	1	—
Writs and Attachments, Register of, ...	1847-9	1	—

24. From the Consolidated Accounting Office:—

Records.	Date.	Vols.	Pris.
Chancery Division Landed (formerly Encumbered) Estates Court:—			
Bank Ledgers (Cash), ...	1868-77	15	—
„ „ (Stock), ...	1864-68	1	—

25.—From the Crown and Hanaper Office:—

Records.	Date.	Vols.	Pris.
Barristers' Oaths Roll, ...	1868-75	—	1
Coroners, Warrants and Writs to elect and supersede, . .	1875	—	1
Exemplifications, Orders for, ...	1873-6	—	1
Great Seal, Commissioners of the, Letters Patent, Commissions and Warrants for Appointment of Lords Justices &c., . .	1875	—	1
Master Extraordinary, Commission for, ...	1840	—	1
Miscellaneous Documents, ...	1875	—	1
Notaries Public, Petitions, Writs and Warrants for appointment of, ...	„	—	1
Oaths, Commissioners of, Petitions and Warrants for appointment of, ...	1875-6	—	1
„ „ Writs of Dedimus for, . .	„	—	1
Parliament, Members of, Warrants for Writs of Election, and Copy Returns, ...	1875	—	1
Peers, Representative, Orders of House of Lords establishing right to vote, ...	„	—	} 1
„ „ Warrants, Writs, Returns and Oaths at Election of, . .	„	—	
Petty Bag Proceedings, Miscellaneous Papers . . .	1857-69	—	} 1
„ „ Writs of Sci. Fa. and Orders for same, .	1875-6	—	

CROWN AND HANAPER OFFICE—*continued.*

Records.	Date.	Vols.	Pris.
Proclamations (Draft), Orders and Warrants for Sealing same,	1876	—	1
Warrants for Commission of Assize and Association,	"	—	1
" " Inquiry and Returns,	"	—	1
" " Justices of the Peace (Counties and Boroughs),	"	—	1
" " Resident Magistrates,	"	—	1
" Superseding and Reinstating Justices of the Peace,	"	—	1
" and Writs of Dedimus, for Justices of the Peace (all Ireland),	"	—	1
" " " " Town Justices,	"	—	1
Writ of ad quod Damnum, Warrant, Writ and Inquisition,	"	—	1
Writs of Dedimus for Justices of the Peace (Counties and Boroughs),	"	—	1
" " " " Queen's Counsel,	"	—	1
" " " " Resident Magistrates,	"	—	1

26. From the Land Judges' Court, Chancery :—

Records.	Date.	Vols.	Preis.
Affidavits,	1875-6	30	—
" Alphabetical List of,	"	1	—
" Numerical List of,	"	1	—
Appearance Book,	"	1	—
Building Leases, Copies of,	"	—	1
Cash Balancing Book,	"	1	—
" Book,	"	1	—
Claims,	"	—	1
Consents and Miscellaneous Documents,	"	—	1
Conveyances, Copies of,	"	—	6
Landlord and Tenant Act :—Statements,	"	—	1
Notices to Tenants (Final),	"	—	6
" " Objections to,	"	—	1
" and Rentals, Index to Objections to,	1874-76	1	—
Orders, Absolute,	1875-6	1	—
" (Church Act),	1874	—	1
" Miscellaneous,	1875-6	1	—
Paymasters' Certificates,	1875	..	1
Petitions,	"	6	—
" (large out of sequence),	1875-6	1	—
" Supplemental,	1875-6	9	—

LAND JUDGES COURT, CHANCERY—continued.

Records.	Date.	Vols.	Pruis.
Record of Proceedings, ...	1875-6	1	—
Rentals (Flanagan), ...	"	3	—
„ (Ormsby), ...	"	5	—
„ Registrar, ...	"	1	—
Sales, Private Proposals, ...	1876	—	1
„ Provincial, Biddings, Rentals, and Auctioneers' Affidavits, .	"	—	1
Schedules of Incumbrances, Draft Final	"	3	—
„ „ Flanagan, ...	1875-6	8	—
" " Ormsby, ...	1875-6	2	—
" " Objections to, Final, . . .	1876	—	1
Solicitors' Registry Book, ...	"	1	—

27. From the Office of Registrar in Lunacy :—

Records.	Date.	Vols.	Pruis.
Accounts, ...	1876	1	—
Affidavits, ...	"	1	—
Petitions and Reports, ...	"	2	—

28. From the Queen's Bench Division :—

Records.	Date.	Vols.	Pruis.
Affidavit Book, ...	1884	1	—
Affidavits, ...	"	6	—
„ Judgment Mortgage, ...	"	1	—
Bills of Sale, ...	"	10	—
„ „ Index to (Alphabetical), . . .	1885-6	1	—
„ „ „ (Numerical), . . .	"	1	—
Cause Books, ...	1886	4	—
„ „ Index to, ...	"	1	—
Executions, ...	"	1	—
Judgment Book, ...	"	1	—
Judgments, ...	"	19	—
Pleadings, ...	"	7	—
Præcipes, ...	"	3	—
„ Index to, ...	1885-6	3	—
Registrar's Certificate Book, ...	1873-85	1	—

29. From the Queen's Bench (late Common Pleas) Division :—

Records.	Date.	Vols.	Pruts.
Affidavit Book, ...	1893	1	—
Affidavits, ...	"	6	—
" Judgments Mortgage, ...	"	1	—
Cause Books, ...	"	3	—
" " Index to, ...	"	1	—
Caveats, ...	1884–5	1	—
Court Books, ...	1889	4	—
Executions, ...	1886–8	3	—
Judgment Books, ...	1885	1	—
Judgments, ...	"	19	—
Pleadings, ...	"	6	—
Præcipes, ...	"	9	—
" Index to, ...	1885–6	1	—
Registrar's Certificate Book, ...	1881–6	1	—
Rule Books, ...	1885	4	—
Warrants, ...	1887–88	1	—
Writs of Summons, ...	1885	37	—

30. From the Exchequer Division :—

Records.	Date.	Vols.	Prts.
Affidavit Book, ...	1888	1	—
Affidavits, ...	"	7	—
Cause Books, ...	"	6	—
" " Index to, ...	"	1	—
Court Books, ...	"	6	—
Judgment Book, ...	"	1	—
Judgments, ...	"	12	—
Orders (Chamber), ...	"	1	—
Pleadings, ...	"	8	—
Præcipes for Executions, ...	"	3	—
Writs of Summons, ...	"	14	—

31. From the Court of Bankruptcy :—

Records.	Date.	Vols.	Prds.
Day List Book, Chief Registrar and Chief Clerk, ...	1878	1	—
Debtors' Summons, ...	"	1	—
Files (Arrangement), ...	"	—	55
„ (Bankruptcy), ...	"	—	57
„ Miscellaneous Arrangement and Bankruptcy Files, . .	"	—	7
Insolvency, Declarations of, ...	"	—	1
Note Books :—			
„ „ Chief Clerk, ...	1875-6	4	—
„ „ „ Registrar, ...	"	3	—
„ „ Registrar, ...	1855-6	1	—
„ „ „ (Doyle), ...	1874-6	5	—
„ „ „ (Fagan), ...	1875	5	—
Parliamentary Returns, ...	"	—	1
Petition Book (Arrangements), ...	1873-6	1	—
„ „ (Bankruptcy), ...	"	1	—
Petitions not proceeded with (Arrangement), . . .	1876	1	—
„ „ „ (Bankruptcy), ...	"	1	—
Precipes on Issuing Execution, ...	"	—	1
Sittings Book (Court), ...	"	1	—

32. From the Principal Probate Registry :—

Records.	Date.	Vols.	Prds.
Affidavits leading to Citations, &c., . . .	1876	—	1
„ of Scripts, ...	"	—	1
Bonds and Papers leading to Grants, ...	"	—	20
Calendar, ...	"	1	—
Caveat Books, ...	1871-5	2	—
Cause Book (setting down), . . .	1868-76	1	—
Contentious Papers, ...	1876	—	1
Grant Books, ...	"	4	—
„ „ (District), ...	"	9	—
Grants, Principal and District Registry, Index to, . . .	"	1	—
Matrimonial Cause Papers, ...	1875-6	—	1
Records (bound), ...	1874-6	1	—
Rule Book (Court), ...	1876	1	—
„ „ Registrar (Keating), . . .	"	1	—
„ „ „ (Wilsy), . . .	1874-6	1	—

PRINCIPAL PROBATE REGISTRY— *continued.*

Records.	Date	Vols.	Frels.
Schedules, ...	1876	9	—
Stamp Office Certificates, ...	"	—	6
Taxed Costs, ...	"	8	—
Will Books, ...	"	3	—
„ „ (District), ...	"	6	—
Wills, ...	"	—	30
„ Unproved, ...	1875-6	—	1
Writ Book, ...	1871-6	1	—

33. From the ARMAGH District Probate Registry :—

Records.	Date	Vols.	Frels.
Administration (Intestate) Papers, ...	1876	—	4
Caveats, ...	1873 & 6	..	1
Wills, ...	1876	—	} 6
„ Unproved, ...	"	—	

34. From the BALLINA District Probate Registry :—

Records.	Date	Vols.	Frels.
Administration (Intestate) Papers, ...	1876	—	3
Wills, ...	"	—	1

35. From the BELFAST District Probate Registry :—

Records.	Date	Vols.	Frels.
Administration (Intestate) Papers, ...	1876	—	4
Caveats, ...	"	—	1
Wills, ...	"	—	} 12
„ Unproved, ...	"	—	

36. From the CAVAN District Probate Registry :—

Records.	Date	Vols.	Frels.
Administration (Intestate) Papers, ...	1876	—	}
Caveats, ...	"	—	} 3
Wills, ...	"	—	}
„ Unproved, ...	"	—	

37. From the CORK District Probate Registry:—

Records.	Date.	Vols.	Pcels.
Administration (Intestate) Papers, ...	1876	—	6
Wills, ...	"	—	1

38. From the KILKENNY District Probate Registry:—

Records.	Date.	Vols.	Pcels.
Administration (Intestate) Papers, ...	1876	—	1
Wills, ...	"	—	1

39. From the LIMERICK District Probate Registry:—

Records.	Date.	Vols.	Pcels.
Administration (Intestate) Papers, ...	1876	—	1
Wills, ...	"	—	2
„ Killaloe and Limerick Diocese, and Limerick District Registry, Index to, ...	1686-1873	1	—

40. From the LONDONDERRY District Probate Registry:—

Records.	Date.	Vols.	Pcels.
Administration (Intestate) Papers, ...	1876	—	2
Grant Book (Intestate), ...	1861-1876	1	—
„ „ (Probate), ...	1868-1876	1	—
Wills, ...	1876	—	1

41. From the MULLINGAR District Probate Registry:—

Records.	Date.	Vols.	Pcels.
Administration (Intestate) Papers, ...	1876	—	1
Wills, ... : .	"	—	1

42. From the TUAM District Probate Registry:—

Records.	Date.	Vols.	Pcels.
Administration (Intestate) Papers, ...	1876	} —	1
Caveats, ...	"		
Wills, ...	"	—	1

43. From the WATERFORD District Probate Registry :—

Records.	Date.	Vals.	Prels.
Administration (Intestate Papers), ...	1576	—	6
Wills	"	} —	7
„ Unproved.	"		

44. From the State Paper Office :—

Records.	Date.	Vals.	Prels.
Chief Secretary's Office :—			
Arms Licence Papers :—			
County Antrim, ...	1830 -37		
„ Armagh, ...	1830-38		
„ Cavan, ...	1830-37		
„ Carlow, ...	1833	—	1
„ Clare, ...	1831-33		
„ Cork, ...	1834-37		
„ Donegal, ...	1835-36		
„ Down, ...	1836-37	} --	1
„ Dublin, ...	"		
„ Fermanagh, ...	1833-37		
„ Galway, ...	1833-37		
„ Kerry, ...	1830-37		
„ Kildare, ...	1835-36	—	1
„ Kilkenny, ...	1835-37		
„ King's, ...	1830-37		
„ Limerick, ...	1835-37		
„ Londonderry, ...	1835-37		
„ Longford, ...	1830-37		
„ Louth, ...	"	—	1
„ Mayo, ...	1835-36		
„ Meath, ...	1831-37		
„ Monaghan, ...	1830-37		
„ Queen's, ...	"		
„ Roscommon, ...	1831-37	—	1
„ Sligo, ...	1836-37		
„ Tipperary, ...	1830, 37		
„ Tyrone, ...	1830-37		
„ Waterford, ...	1832-37		
„ Westmeath, ...	1833-37	} —	1
„ Wexford, ...	1831-37		
„ Wicklow, ...	"		

STATE PAPER OFFICE—*continued.*

Records.	Date.	Vols.	Prels.
Chief Secretary's Office :—			
Arms (Firearms), Returns of Repairs and Sales, . . .	1822-23	—	29
Board of Health, Register of Letters, &c., ...	1832	—	1
Cholera Reports :—			
" (Parishes or Places), ...	1832-34	—	46
" (Central Board), ...	1832	—	1
Gunmakers, Index Book, ...	1831-32	1	—
Gunpowder Acts, Papers relating to, . . .	1793-1839	—	1
" Certificates for Purchasers, . . .	1831-32	—	1
" Index Book, ...	1831-32	1	—
Gunpowder Licences (Papers) :—			
County Antrim, ...	1826-37	—	7
" Armagh, ...	1826-38	—	5
" Carlow, ...	1826-37	—	1
" Cavan, ...	1834-37	—	2
" Clare, ...	1834-35	—	8
" Cork (City), ...	1834-37	—	7
" Cork, ...	1833-37	—	10
" Donegal, ...	1836-37	—	4
" Down, ...	1835-37	—	8
" Dublin (City), ...	1817-37	—	10
" Dublin, ...	1834-37	—	7
" Fermanagh, ...	1833-37	—	4
" Galway, ...	1833-37	—	4
" Kerry, ...	1835-37	—	4
" Kildare, ...	1834-37	—	4
" Kilkenny, ...	"	—	7
" King's, ...	"	—	5
" Leitrim, ...	"	—	3
" Limerick (City), . . .	"	—	6
" Limerick, ...	1797-1837	—	8
" Londonderry, . . .	1834-37	—	4
" Longford, ...	"	—	8
" Louth, ...	"	—	4
" Mayo, ...	"	—	4
" Meath, ...	"	—	3
" Monaghan, ...	"	—	7
" Queen's, ...	1833-37	—	6
" Roscommon, ...	1819-37	—	8

STATE PAPER OFFICE—*continued.*

Records.	Date	Vols	Prels.
Chief Secretary's Office :—			
Gunpowder Licences (Papers) :—			
County Sligo, ...	1834–37	—	3
„ Tipperary, ...	„	—	6
„ Tyrone, ...	„	—	4
„ Waterford, ...	„	—	5
„ Westmeath, ...	1833–37	—	4
„ Wexford, ...	1834–37	—	6
„ Wicklow, ...	„	—	4
Gunpowder Licences, Papers (2nd Series), . . .	1843–62	—	70
„ „ Importations, and Seizures, Papers relating to,	1821–35	—	2
„ „ Register, ...	1831–5	1	—
„ „ „	1832–37	2	—
„ „ Vendors and Spirit Dealers, . . .	1834–36	—	1
Lord Lieutenant, Patent appointing the Earl of Northumberland, ...	1763	—	1
Private Official Letter Books, ...	1825–1788	18	..
Relief of Distress, Ireland, 1822 :—			
Applications for Relief, and Reports :—			
Co. Clare and Limerick, ...	⎫		
„ Galway, ...	⎬ 1822	—	3
„ King's, Mayo, Roscommon, and others, . .	⎭		
Applications for Relief, Register of, . . .	„	2	—
Fever Reports and Medical Aid, ...	„	—	1
Letter Book of Commissioners, ...	„	—	—
Letters and Papers, Committees, London, &c., . .	„	—	1
Potatoes and Oatmeal, Purchase and Distribution of,	„	—	1
Sums issued for Relief, Register of, . . .	„	1	—
State of the Poor, Ireland, 1824 :—			
Agricultural Labourers and Employment — Reports of Evidence at Public Inquiry Courts, ...	1835	—	3
Analysis of Laws affecting the Poor, . . .	1834	—	1
Evidence at Public Inquiry Courts, Reports of, .	„	—	3
Irish in Great Britain, Returns from Roman Catholic Clergy on the condition of the, ...	„	—	1
Surveys and Maps :—			
Cork and Blackrock Navigation, ...	1835	⎫	
County Cork, ...	1811	⎪	
Dublin Bay, ...	1800	⎬ —	8
Galway Bay, Harbours, ...	1822	⎪	
Lough Corrib, ...	1837	⎭	

STATE PAPER OFFICE—*continued.*

Records.	Date.	Vols.	Pmls.
Chief Secretary's Office (Military Department):—			
Army Account Book, ...	1823–29	1	—
Army Accounts :—			
Commissary-General's, ...	1803–3	—	1
Commissioner's (Mr. Hall's), ...	1814–18	—	1
Military Accountants, Lists of, ...	1821	—	1
Regimental and General Officers', . . .	1824	—	1
Commissions, Lists of, ...	1811–18	—	1
Deaths and Desertions, ...	1811–18	—	1
Estimates, ...	1797	—	1
Gold and Silver Coinage, ...	1820	—	1
Hompesch's Dragoon Riflemen, Adjutant's Book, . .	1799–1802	3	—
Illegal Marriages and Political Addresses of Roman Catholic Clergymen, ...	1822–29	—	1
Letters :—			
Commander of the Forces and his Secretary, . .	1804–7 / 1819–28	—	19
Commissarial Department, ...	1833	4	1
Departmental, ...	1819–23	—	2
Line, ...	1827, 1830	—	1
Military Account Office, ...	1831	—	1
Quarter Master General, ...	1801–7	—	1
Secretaries of War and State, . . .	1818–30	—	18
Regimental Paymasters' Appointments, Register of, . .	1798–1828	—	1
Richbell's Regiment Muster Rolls, ...	1748–54	—	1
Schedules of Accounts, Books, and Documents of Military Records of Ireland deposited in Office of Commissioners of Military Accounts, 1831. . . .	1822	—	1
Chief Secretary's Office, Military Department (Militia Branch):—			
Arms, ...	1814, 1823	—	1
Accounts, ...	1797–1828	—	1
Civil Power, employment of Staff in aid of, . .	1818	—	1
Clothing, ...	1813–28	—	1
Depôts, ...	1818–29	—	1
Correspondence relative to :—			
Armagh, ...	1816–28		
Carlow, ...	1827–27		
Cavan, ...	1815–29	—	1
Clare, ...	1815–17		
Cork (North, South, and City), . .	1815–30		
Donegal, ...	1815–25		
Down (North and South), . .	1815–28	—	1
Dublin (City and County), . .	1815–18		

STATE PAPER OFFICE—*continued.*

Records.	Date.	Vols.	Price.
Chief Secretary's Office, Military Department (Militia Branch) :—			
Depôts, Correspondence relative to :—			
Fermanagh, ...	1815-25		
Galway, ... , ...	1810, 1814-29		
Kerry, ...	1815-17		
Kildare, ...	1814-34	—	1
Kilkenny, ...	1815-37		
King's Co., ...	1815-36		
Leitrim, ...	1814-35		
Limerick (County and City), . . .	1815-32		
Longford, ...	1815-34		
Louth, ...	1814-1817		
Mayo (South), ...	1817	—	1
Meath, ...	1816-37		
Monaghan, ...	1815-17		
Sligo, ...	1814-30		
Tipperary, ...	1817-37		
Waterford, ...	1815-37	—	1
Wexford, ...	1815-37		
Wicklow, ...	1815-17		
Disembodying Regiments, Papers relating to, . . .	1816	—	1
Estimates, ...	1811-29	—	1
Half-pay Officers, ...	1815-29	—	1
Letters from Commander of Forces, . . .	1809-13	—	8
Line, Volunteers to.	1804-23	—	1
Memorials, &c., of Officers, . . .	1819-31	—	7
Militia Bill, Copies and Proposed Amendments, . .	1815	—	1
„ Purposes, Monies raised in Counties, .	1803-23	—	1
Papers re Militia Regiment, Galway, . . .	1807-15		1
„ „ „ „ Kildare, ...	1808		1
„ „ „ „ Wicklow, ...	1798-1825	—	1
„ Miscellaneous, ...	1797-1829	—	1
Paymasters, ...	1811-29	—	1
Printed Forms (Acts, Instructions, and Regulations), .	1804-23	—	1
Quarter Master Ring, Case of, . . .	1825-26	—	1
Recruiting and Returns, ...	1803-16	—	1
Chief Secretary's Office, Yeomanry Department :—			
Account Books :—			
Ledger, ...	1797-99	1	—

STATE PAPER OFFICE—*continued.*

Records.	Date.	Vols.	Print.
Chief Secretary's Office, Yeomanry Department :—			
Account Books :—			
Pay Books (Permanent Duty), ...	1798–1832	6	—
Staff Book (Brigade Majors), ...	1810–12	1	—
Addresses or Direction Book, ...	—	1	—
Arms Books, ...	1814–21	8	—
„ Returns, ...	1828, 1831	—	1
Augmentation of or raising Corps, Proposal Book, . .	1810–14, 1834	2	—
Clothing Allowance Books, ...	1797–1829	4	—
County Corps Papers, ...	1798–1829	—	8
Effectives Book, ...	—	—	1
Establishment Alteration Book, ...	1809–15	1	—
„ Books, ...	}—1810{ 1810–18	} 2	—
„ „ (Supplemental) . . .	1833	1	—
Exercise and Inspection Books, ...	1803–29	5	—
Horse Furniture Repairs, ...	1810–18	—	1
Miscellaneous Papers (with list of Corps), . . .	1802–19	—	1
Office Books :—			
Attendance, and Letter Despatch Book, . . .	1814	1	—
Documents' Corrections Book, ...	1810–24	1	—
Instruction and Letter Minute Book, . .	1830–31	1	—
Reference Books, ...	1807–43	4	—
Weekly State of Work, ...	1806–7	1	—
Orders, General Agent, ...	1811–43	—	1
Permanent Serjeants Books, ...	1808, 1818	2	—
Record of Yeomanry, Ireland, ...	1823–43	—	1
Chief Secretary's Office and Council Office :—			
Miscellaneous Papers, ...	1700–90	—	16
Council Office :—			
Maps of Unions of Parishes :—			
Burnchurch (3) Diocese of Ossory, . . .			
Castlecomer, „ „ „ . .			
Kilmanagh, „ „ Ross, . .	} 1834–45	—	1
Kengo, „ „ Dromore, . .			
Papers connected with Unions or Divisions of Parishes, and changes of titles of Churches, ...	} 1821–1845	—	80
Armagh · Waterford, ...			
Returns, Reports, and Rules, Unions of Parishes, . .	1799–1844	—	1

45. From the Quit Rent Office :—

Records.	Date.	Vols.	Pro's.
Twopenny Books, ...	1876-7	16	—

46. From the Crown and Peace Office of the county of Armagh :—

Records.	Date.	Vols.	Pro's.
Appeals to Assizes, ...	1876	—	1
Arms Licence Application Lists, ...	1876-78	—	1
Civil Bill Books, ...	1825-78	8	—
„ Papers, ...	1876	—	1
Constables (High), Bonds and Warrants, . .	„	—	1
Coroners' Inquests, ...	Jan.-June, 1878	—	1
Crown Files at Assizes, ...	1878	—	1
„ „ „ Quarter Sessions, ...	„	—	1
Fines Account Book, ...	1868-78	1	—
Jurors' Lists, ...	1876	—	1
Landlord and Tenant (1870) Act: Papers, . .	„	—	1
Maps, Plans, Awards, &c., ...	„	—	1
Pawnbrokers' Bonds, ...	„	—	1
Presentments, ...	„	—	4
Presentment Books, ...	„	2	—
Query Books, ...	„	4	—
Renewal Affidavits, ...	„	—	1
Voters' Lists, ...	„	—	1

47. From the Crown and Peace Office of the county of Carlow:—

Records.	Date.	Vols.	Pro's.
Coroners' Inquests, ...	1876-78	—	1
Crown Files at Assizes, ...	1876	—	1
„ and Civil Files at Quarter Sessions, ...	„	—	1

48. From the Crown and Peace Office of the county of Cavan:—

Records.	Date.	Vols.	Prels.
Appeals to Assizes,	1876	—	1
Civil Bill Book,	1875-76	1	—
„ „ Papers,	1876	—	1
Coroners' Inquests,	1874-76	—	1
Crown Files at Assizes,	1876	—	1
„ „ „ Quarter Sessions,	„	—	1
Gaol Contractor's Bond,	1875	—	1
Jurors' Books,	1876	2	—
„ Lists,	1876-76	—	1
Landlord and Tenant (1870) Act; Papers,	1876	—	1
Maps, Plans, Awards, &c.,	„	—	2
Miscellaneous,	„	—	1
Presentment Books,	1875, 1876	2	—
Process Server's Book,	1875-76	1	—
Publicans' Licence Notices,	1876	—	1
Voters' Lists, Claims, and Objections,	„	—	1
„ Registers,	„	—	1

49. From the Crown and Peace Office of the county of Down:—

Records.	Date.	Vols.	Prels.
Belfast Harbour Commissioners' Accounts,	1876	—	1
Civil Bill Books,	1875-76	2	—
Crown Book at Quarter Sessions,	1867-75	1	—
„ Files	1876	—	1
Ejectment Book,	1855-76	1	—
Freemasons' Memorials,	1876	—	1
Jurors' Lists,	1875-76	—	4
Landlord and Tenant (1870) Act; Papers,	1876	—	1
Maps, Plans, Awards, &c.,	1875-76	—	5
Presentments,	1875-76	—	4
Presentment Books,	1875	2	—
Query Books,	„	3	—
Renewal Affidavits,	„	—	1
Voters' Lists,	„	—	1

50. From the Crown Office, county and city of Dublin :—

Records.	Date.	Vols.	Prels.
Crown Book (City), ...	1870-4	1	—
„ Files, ...	1876	—	6

51. From the Peace Office of the county of Dublin :—

Records.	Date.	Vols.	Prels.
Appeals from Quarter Sessions, ...	1872-76	—	1
„ to „ „	1873-76	—	1
Civil Bill Books, ...	1822-76	9	—
„ „ Papers, ...	1820-76	—	1
Convictions, Records of, ...	1876	—	1
Fines and Estreats, ...	.	—	1
Jurors' Petitions and Declarations, . . . : .	1868-76	—	1
Jury Panels, ...	1874-76	—	1
Landlord and Tenant (1870) Act : Papers, . . .	1871-76	—	1
Magistrates' and Cess Payers' Declarations, . . .	1876	—	1
Maps, ...	1868-76	—	6
Publicans' Licence Register, ...	1873-76	1	—
Renewal Affidavits, ...	1875-76	—	1
Summons and Plaints, ...	1874-76	—	1
Voters' Registers and Lists, ...	.	22	—
„ Registration Appeals and Papers, . . .	1868-76	—	1

52. From the Peace Office, county of the city of Dublin :—

Records	Date.	Vols.	Prels.
Appeals, ...	1876	} —	1
Convictions, ...	„		
Crown Files, ...	„	—	2
Freemasons' Registry, ...	1845, 1846	—	1
Jurors' Lists, ...	1876	4	—
Maps, Plans, Specifications, Awards, &c., . . .	.	—	1
Publicans' Licence Notices, ...	.	—	1
Voters' Lists, ...	.	20	—

58. From the Crown and Peace Office of the county of Fermanagh :—

Records.	Date.	Vols.	Pcds.
Appeals to Assizes, ...	1876	—	1
Civil Bill Books, ...	"	6	—
„ „ Papers, ...	"	—	1
Crown Files at Assizes, ...	"	—	1
„ „ „ Quarter Sessions, ...	1875-76	—	1
Enrolment Book, ...	1864-76	1	—
Landlord and Tenant (1870) Act: Papers, . . .	1876	—	1
„ „ „ „ Record of Claim and Dispute Book, ...	1871-76	1	—
Process Servers' Appointments, ...	1875	—	1
Presentment and Query Books, ...	"	2	—
Voters' Register, ...	"	1	—

54. From the Crown and Peace Office of the county of Kerry :—

Records.	Date.	Vols.	Pcds.
Appeals to Assizes, ...	1876	—	1
Arms License Application Lists, ...	1875-76	—	1
Civil Bill Books, ...	1876	6	—
„ „ Papers, ...	"	—	1
Coroner's Election Qualification, ...	"	—	1
Crown Files at Assizes, ...	"	—	1
„ „ „ Quarter Sessions, ...	"	—	1
Fishery Papers, ...	"	—	1
Jurors' Books, ...	"	2	—
„ Lists, ...	"	—	1
Landlord and Tenant (1870) Act: Books, . . .	1870-76	2	—
„ „ „ „ Papers, ...	1875	—	1
Magistrates' and Oes Payers' Declarations, . . .	1875-76	—	1
Maps, Plans, Awards, &c., ...	1876	—	1
Militia Returns, ...	1875-76	—	1
Polling Districts Order Book, ...	1877	1	—
Presentment Books, ...	1875	10	—
Presentments, ...	"	—	2
Publicans' License Application Book, ...	1869-75	1	—
„ „ Notices, ...	1875-76	—	1
Renewal Affidavits, ...	1875	—	1
Sessions (Petty) Districts Papers, ...	"	—	1
Voters' Registers and Lists, ...	"	—	1

55. From the Crown and Peace Office of the county of Kildare :—

Records.	Date.	Vols.	Pcts.
Appeals to Assizes, ...	1875-76	—	1
Civil Bill Papers, ...	»	—	1
Coroners' Inquests, ...	1876	—	1
Crown Files at Assizes, ...	1875-76	—	2
„ „ Quarter Sessions	1876	—	1
Jurors' Books, ...	1875-76	2	—
„ Lists, ...	1875	—	1
Landlord and Tenant (1870) Act : Papers, . .	1874-76	—	1
Maps, Plans, Awards, &c., ...	1876	—	1
Petitions, ...	1876	—	1
Probate Papers	1875-76	—	1
Presentments, ...	1876	—	2
Proclamations, ...	»	—	1
Publicans' Licence Notices, ...	1875-76	—	6
„ „ Registers, ...	1875-76	—	1
Quary Books, ...	1876	2	—
Removal Affidavits, ...	»	—	1
Reports, ...	1865-61	—	1
Voters' Registers, Lists, &c., ...	1871-76	—	2

56. From the Crown and Peace Office of the King's county :—

Records.	Date.	Vols.	Pcts.
Civil Bill Books, ...	1875-76	0	—
„ „ Papers, ...	1876	—	1
Coroners' Inquests, ...	1875-76	—	1
Crown Files at Assizes, ...	1876	—	1
„ „ „ Quarter Sessions, ...	»	—	1
Presentment Memorials, ...	»	—	1
Jurors' Lists, ...	»	—	1
Landlord and Tenant (1870) Act : Papers, . . .	»	—	1
Magistrates' and Cess Payers' Declarations, . . .	»	—	1
Maps, Plans, Awards, &c., ...	»	—	1
Presentment Books, ...	»	2	—
Presentment Papers, ...	»	—	1
Publicans' Notices, Lists, &c., ...	»	—	1
Removal Affidavits, ...	»	—	1
Returns and Orders (Government), ...	»	—	1
Voters' Registers, Lists, &c.…	»	3	1

57. From the Crown and Peace Office of the county and city of Limerick:—

Records.	Date.	Vols.	Pacls.
Appeals to Assizes, ...	1876	—	1
Arms License Application Lists, ...	"	—	1
Civil Bill Book, ...	1875-76	1	—
" Papers, ...	1876	—	1
Convictions (Summary), ...	1851-76	—	1
Coroners' Inquests, ...	1876	—	1
Crown Files at Assizes, ...	"	—	1
" " Quarter Sessions, ...	"	—	1
Fines, Jurors, Affidavits to remit, ...	"	—	1
Fishery Papers, ...	"	—	1
Freemasons' and Friendly Brothers' Memorials. . .	"	—	1
Grand Jury Bill Book, ...	1870-71	1	—
Jurors' Books, ...	1876	2	—
Landlord and Tenant (1870) Act Papers, . . .	"	—	1
Maps, Plans, Awards, &c., ...	"	—	4
Poor Law Guardians' (ex officio) Return, . .	1875-76	—	1
Presentment Books, ...	1876	20	—
Presentments, ...	"	—	4
Publicans' License Notices, ...	"	—	1
" " Renewal Certificates Register, . .	"	1	—
Quarry Book, ...	"	1	—
Renewal Affidavits, ...	"	—	1
Session (Petty) Clerks' Election Papers, . .	"	—	1
Voters' Lists, ...	"	—	1

58. From the Crown and Peace Office of the county of Londonderry:—

Records.	Date.	Vols.	Pacls.
Appeals to Assizes, ...	1876	—	1
Civil Bill Books, ...	1875-76	3	—
" Papers, ...	1876	—	1
Coroners' Inquests, ...	1875-76	—	2
Crown Files at Assizes, ...	1876	—	1
" " " Quarter Sessions, . .	"	—	1
Fishery Papers, ...	"	—	1
Jurors' Book, ...	"	1	—
" Lists, ...	"	—	1

CROWN AND PEACE OFFICE, COUNTY OF LONDONDERRY—con.

Records.	Date.	Vols.	Prols.
Landlord and Tenant (1870) Act; Papers, ...	"	—	1
Loan Fund (Kilrea) Rule, ...	"	—	1
Magistrates' and Cess Payers' Declarations, ...	"	~	1
Presentment Books, ...	"	15	~
Presentments, ...	"	—	8
Process Servers' Books	1865-76	3	—
Voters' Registers (Copy), Lists, Claims, and Objections, .	1878	9	—

59. From the Crown and Peace Office of the county of Longford :—

Records.	Date.	Vols.	Prols.
Civil Bill Papers, ...	1878	—	1
Coroners' Inquests, ...	"	~	1
Crown Files at Assizes, ...	"	—	1
" " " Quarter Sessions, ...	"	—	1
Presentment Books, ...	"	1	—
Query Books, ...	"	1	—

60. From the Crown and Peace Office of the county of Louth :—

Records.	Date.	Vols.	Prols.
Carlingford Lough Commissioners' Accounts, ...	1876	—	1
Civil Bill Papers, ...	"	~	1
Coroners' Inquests, ...	1876-78	~	1
Crown Files at Assizes, ...	1878	—	1
" " " Quarter Sessions, ...	"	—	1
Jurors' Books, ...	"	1	—
" Lists, ...	"	—	1
Magistrates' and Cess Payers' Declarations, ...	"	~	1
Maps, Plans, Awards, &c., ...	"	—	1
Presentment Book, ...	1875-76	1	—
" (undischarged) Book, . . .	1873-74	1	—
Presentments, ...	1876	—	2
Publicans' Licence Notices, ...	1875-6	—	1
" " Register and Application Book, . .	1865-76	1	—
Voters' Lists, ...	1835-49	—	1
" (Copy) Registers, ...	1878	—	1

61. From the Crown and Peace Office of the county of Mayo:—

Records.	Date.	Vols.	Preis.
Appeals to Assizes, ...	1876	—	1
Appeal Book to Quarter Sessions, ...	1878-79	1	—
Capias Book (Assizes), ...	2861-7d	1	—
Civil Bill Books, ...	1874-76	2	—
„ „ Papers, ...	1877	—	1
Coroners' Inquests, ...	1875-76	—	1
Crown Books at Assizes, ...	1876	2	—
„ Files „ „	„	—	1
„ Books „ Quarter Sessions	1875-79	2	—
„ Files „ „	1876	—	1
Deputy Lieutenants' Qualifications, ...	„	—	1
Ejectment Book, ...	1874-76	1	—
Fishery Papers, ...	1876	—	1
Freemasons' Memorials, ...	„	—	1
Jurors' Lists, ...	„	—	1
Landlord and Tenant (1876) Act: Papers, . . .	„	—	1
Maps, Plans, Awards, &c., ...	„	—	1
Militia Returns, ...	„	—	1
Miscellaneous Papers, ...	—	—	1
Presentment Books, ...	1876	28	—
„ and Query Books, ...	„	6	—
Proclamation, ...	„	—	1
Process Servers' Books	„	31	—
Publicans' Lists and Notices, ...	1875-76	—	1
Removal Affidavits, ...	„	—	1
Returns and Correspondence, ...	1876	—	1
Voters' Registers and Lists, ...	„	—	1

62. From the Crown and Peace Office of the county of Meath:—

Records.	Date.	Vols.	Preis.
Appeals to Assizes, ...	1874-76	—	1
Civil Bill Book, ...	1872-75	1	—
„ Papers, ...	1875-76	—	1
Convictions at Petty Sessions, ...	1869-75	—	1
Coroners' District Papers, ...	1872	—	1
Crown Books at Quarter Sessions (Trim), . .	1873-75	1	—
„ Files at Assizes, ...	1876	—	1
„ „ Quarter Sessions (Trim), . . .	„	—	1
Landlord and Tenant (1876) Act: Papers, . .	1871-76	—	1
Maps, Plans, Awards, &c., ...	1874-76	—	1

63. From the Crown Office of the county of Monaghan:—

Records.	Date.	Vols.	Prcls.
Assize Papers received in Crown Office, Registers of,	1836-76	3	—
Copies Books,	1765-1873	3	—
Clerk of the Crown's Patent,	1833	—	1
Coroners' Inquests,	1735-1870	—	13
Crown Books at Assizes,	1727-1876	96	—
„ Files „	1763-1873	—	71
Fines Account (Officers') Book at Assizes,	1853-68	1	—
Monaghan Gaol (Deed of Conveyance),	1811	—	1
Pardon, Grants of,	1773-1834	—	1
Presentment Book (Accounting Affidavits, Receipts Book),	1813-12	1	—
„ Books,	1772-1876	129	—
„ Papers,	1788 1876	—	17
Query and Presentment Book,	1780-48	1	—
„ Books,	1771-1876	13	—
Treasurers' Accounts,	1733-1869	11	—

64. From the Peace Office of the county of Monaghan:—

Records.	Date.	Vols.	Prcls.
Accounts (Clerk of the Peace),	1853-76	—	1
Accounts and Reports,	1857-76	—	1
Appeals to Assizes,	1819-76	—	8
Arms License Application (Court) Books,	1843-45	3	1
„ Applications, Lists of,	1844-5, 1875	—	1
„ Notices (or Applications), Gardiansen, &c.,	1833-46	—	8
„ Registers,	1798-1845	18	—
Attorneys' Accounts,	1853-65	—	1
„ List of,	1853-76	—	1
Bailiffs' Bonds and Appointments,	1857-71	—	1
Copies Books,	1773-25.6	6	—
Census Return Paper,	1831	—	1
Civil Bill Books,	1796-1876	228	—
„ (Assistant Barristers),	1833-76	133	—
„ Papers (Miscellaneous),	1835-76	—	3
Clerk of the Peace's Affidavits,	1854-56	—	1
Constable (High), Appointment and Bond,	1853	—	1
Constabulary Papers,	1854-55	—	1
Convictions (Summary),	1844-76	—	1
Convictions and Appeals (to Quarter Sessions),	1855-76	—	4
Coroners' Election Papers,	1857	—	1
Crown Books at Quarter Sessions,	1833-67	13	—
„ Files „	1773-1876	—	6

PEACE OFFICE, COUNTY MONAGHAN—continued.

Records.	Date.	Vols.	Puds.
Deputy Clerk of the Peace's Affidavits and Appointments, .	1851-78	—	1
„ Lieutenants' Appointments and Qualifications, .	1833-61	—	1
Ejectments, Affidavits to verify, , ...	1819-61	—	8
Ejectment Books, ...	1817-76	16	1
Election of M.P.'s, Indentures of, ...	1830-59	—	1
„ Papers, ...	1832-74	—	1
Fines, Affidavits to reduce, ...	1833-76	—	1
„ Books, ...	1839-61	2	—
„ (Petty Sessions) Lists, ...	1838-62	—	1
Fishery Papers, ...	1854-74	—	1
Freeholders' Affidavits, ...	1768-1849	—	8
„ Application Court Books, . . .	1833-39	2	—
„ „ Lists of, . . .	1833	1	—
„ Registers, ...	1768-1846	17	—
„ Registration Sessions Books, . .	1830-38	3	—
Freemasons' Memorials, ...	1830-61	—	1
Friendly Society Rules, ...	1834	—	1
Gaol Governors' Bonds and Appointments, . .	1856-76	—	1
„ (Clones Bridewell) Papers, ...	1856-67	—	1
Grand Jury Bill Books, ...	1751-1857	16	—
Gunpowder Certificates, ...	1836-43	—	1
Informations and Recognizances, Lists of, . .	1836-44	1	1
Insolvency Papers, ...	1811-78	—	1
Jurors' Books, ...	1833-73	17	—
„ Lists, ...	1830-76	—	8
„ Revision List Papers, ...	1840-62	—	1
Landlord and Tenant (1870) Act : Papers and Books, .	1870-76	2	2
Leases and Deeds, ...	1798-1849	—	1
Legacy Books	1837-76	5	—
„ and Probate Papers, ...	1833-76	—	1
Loan Fund Rules, ...	1838-59	—	1
Magistrates' Commissions, ...	1768-1873	—	1
„ Lists and Papers, ...	1833-69	—	1
„ Writs of Dedimus, . . .	1770-1833	—	1
„ „ Supersedeas, . . .	1823-73	—	1
Magistrates' and Cess Payers' Declarations at Road Sessions,	1819-76	—	4
Manorial Court Papers, ...	1839-63	—	1
Manorial Patents (6 James I.—1 James II.), . . .	1608-85	—	1
Maps, Plans, Awards, &c., ...	1833-75	13	18
Meetinghouse (Religious) Notice, ...	1846	—	1
Militia Papers, ...	1768-1873	—	1
Miscellaneous, ...	—	—	1

PEACE OFFICE, COUNTY MONAGHAN—*continued.*

Records.	Date.	Vols.	Prcls.
Oaths of Allegiance,	1797–1833	—	1
Orders (or Posting (Assistant Barrister),	1826, 1845	2	—
Poll Books,	1783, 1818–85	42	—
Polling Districts Papers,	1852–72	—	1
Poor Law Commissioners' Orders and ex-officio Guardian Certificates,	1839–57	—	1
Poundkeeper's Bond,	1839–60	—	1
Precedent Book,	—	1	—
Prisoners' Calendars,	1831–72	—	1
Process Servers' Books,	1841–74	10	—
" Papers,	1830–72	—	1
Proclamations,	1851–76	—	2
Receipts,	1826–75	—	1
Recognizance Registers,	1830–43	2	—
Renewal (Decrees) Affidavits,	1818–76	—	12
" Books,	1805–46	5	—
Replevin "	1837–76	2	—
" Papers,	1833–76	—	1
Returns and Orders (Government, &c.), and Correspondence,	1815–75	—	1
Roman Catholic Qualification Oath Register,	1825–30	1	—
Sacrament Certificates,	1765–80	—	1
Savings Bank Rules,	1834–48	—	1
Sessions (Petty) Civil Register,	1838–82	1	—
" Criminal "	1833–80	1	—
" Clerks' Papers,	1843–68	—	1
" District "	1838–71	—	1
" Summons Registers,	1788–84	2	—
Sheriff (High), Patent of Appointment,	1789	—	1
Spirit Licence Application (Court) Book,	1833–83	1	—
" Notices or Applications, Affidavits of Sureties, &c.,	1815–76	—	7
Spirit Licence Registers,	1830–83	4	—
" Retailers' Register,	1853–83	1	—
Summons and Plaints,	1870–76	—	1
Tithe Cases Register,	1834	1	—
" Owners' Memorials and Schedules,	1833, 1834	16	—
" Papers,	1832–46	—	1
Tolls and Customs Schedules,	1815–30	—	1
Trees, Affidavits to Register,	1843–64	—	1
Voters' Notices of Claim, Lists of,	1834	—	3
" Objections thereto, and Certificates,	1833–76	—	16
" (Copy) Registers and Lists,	1850–70	—	14
" " " (bound),	"	153	—

PEACE OFFICE, COUNTY MONAGHAN—continued.

Records.	Date.	Vols.	Proh.
Voters' Registration Papers, ...	1868-78	—	1
Weighmasters' and Ballastmasters' Bonds, Oaths, and Appointments, ...	1813-53	—	1
Weights and Measures Papers, ...	1875-58	—	1
„ „ Register, ...	1858-57	1	—
Witnesses' Expenses, ...	1848-74	—	1

65. From the Crown and Peace Office of the Queen's county :—

Records.	Date.	Vols.	Proh.
Arms Licence Application Lists, ...	1875-78	—	1
Civil Bill Papers, ...	1876	—	1
Coroners' Inquests, ...	„	—	1
Crown Files at Assizes, ...	„	—	1
„ „ Quarter Sessions, . . .	„	—	1
Ejectment Book, ...	1873-78	1	—
Fishery Papers, ...	1874-75	—	1
Freemasons' Memorials, . . .	1876	—	1
Jurors' Lists, ...	„	—	1
Landlord and Tenant (1870) Act : Papers, . .	„	—	1
Loan Fund Rules, ...	1876, 1873	—	1
Magistrates' and Com Payers' Declarations, .	1875-76	—	1
Maps, Plans, Awards, &c., . . .	1876	—	1
Presentments, ...	„	—	1
Publicans' Licence Notices, . . .	„	—	1
Quarry Book, ...	„	1	—
Renewal Affidavits, ...	„	—	1
Voters' Registers, Lists, &c., . . .	„	—	1

66. From the Crown and Peace Office of the county of Roscommon :—

Records.	Date.	Vols.	Proh.
Civil Bill Books, ...	1868-75	8	—
Crown Files at Assizes, ...	1876	—	1
„ „ Quarter Sessions, . .	„	—	1
Ejectment Processes, ...	1874-1876	—	1
Jurors' Lists, ...	1876	—	1
Publicans' Licence Notices, . . .	„	—	1
Renewal Affidavits, ...	1874-1876	—	1
Town Commissioners' Accounts, . .	1874-78	—	1

67. From the Crown and Peace Office of the county of Sligo :—

Records.	Date.	Vols.	Pres.
Appeals to Assizes, ...	1876	—	1
Arms Licence Application Lists, ...	"	—	1
Civil Bill Books, ...	"	8	—
Coroners' Inquests, ...	"	—	1
Crown Files at Assizes.	"	—	1
„ „ „ Quarter Sessions, ...	"	—	1
Jurors' Books, ...	"	8	—
„ Lists	"	—	1
Magistrates' and Cess Payers' Declarations, . .	"	—	1
Miscellaneous, ...	1874-76	—	1
Presentment Books, ...	1876	7	—
Presentments, ...	"	—	1
„ (Abstract) Book, ...	"	1	—
Publicans' Licence Notices, ...	"	—	1
Query Book, ...	"	1	—
Removal Affidavits, ...	"	—	1
Voters' Register and Lists, ...	"	1	—

68. From the Crown and Peace Office of the county of Tipperary :—

Records.	Date.	Vols.	Pres.
Appeals to Assizes, ...	1875-76	—	1
Civil Bill Books, ...	1876	4	—
Coroners' Inquests, ...	1874-76	—	1
Crown Files at Assizes, ...	1876	—	1
„ „ „ Quarter Sessions, ...	"	—	1
Enrolment Papers, ...	"	—	1
Freemasons' Memorials, ...	1873-75	—	1
Jurors' Books, ...	1876	7	—
„ Lists, ...	"	—	1
Landlord and Tenant (1870) Act Papers, . .	1870-76	—	1
Presentment Papers, ...	1876	—	6
Removal Affidavits, ...	"	—	1
„ Book, ...	1874-76	1	—
Voters' Lists and Claims, ...	1876	—	1
„ Registers, ...	"	8	—

69. From the Crown and Peace Office of the county of Westmeath :—

Records.	Date.	Vols.	Prts.
Civil Bill Papers, ...	1878	—	1
Coroners' Inquests, ...	1875-6	—	1
Crown Files at Assizes, ...	1878	..	1
„ „ „ Quarter Sessions,	„	—	1
Freemasons' Memorial, ...	„	—	1
Jurors' Books, ...	„	3	—
Landlord and Tenant (1870) Act : Papers,. .	„	—	1
Presentment Books, ...	„	8	—
Presentments, ...	„	—	1
Proclamations, ...	„	—	1
Publicans' Licence Notices, ...	„	—	1
Query Books, ...	„	3	—
Sessions (Petty) Districts Papers, ...	1875-76	—	1

70. From the Crown and Peace Office of the county of Wexford :—

Records.	Date.	Vols.	Prts.
Appeals to Assizes, ...	1876	—	1
Civil Bill Books	1875-76	3	—
„ „ and Ejectment Books, ...	1871-76	3	—
Convictions (Summary), ...	1871-73	—	1
Coroners' Inquests, ...	1875-76	—	1
Crown Files at Assizes, ...	1876	—	1
„ „ „ Quarter Sessions, ...	„	..	1
Ejectment Processes, ...	„	—	1
Fishery Papers, ...	„	—	1
Jurors Books, ...	1875-76	6	—
„ Lists, ...	1876	—	1
Magistrates' Attendance Lists, ...	„	—	1
Maps, Plans, Awards, &c., ...	1875-76	—	1
Militia Papers, ...	873-76	—	1
Presentment Books, ...	1876	8	—
Presentments, ...	„	—	1
Publicans' Licence Notices, ...	1875-76	—	1
Query Books, ...	1876	4	—
Renewal Affidavits, ...	„	—	1

71. From the Crown and Peace Office of the county of Wicklow:—

Records.	Date.	Vols.	Preta.
Civil Bill Papers, ...	1575	—	1
Coroners' Inquests, ...	1575-78	—	1
County Cess Applotment Books, . . .	1823-73	84	—
Crown Files at Assizes, ...	1575	—	1
„ „ „ Quarter Sessions, . . .	„	—	1
Freeholders' Memorials, ...	„	—	1
Jurors' Lists, ...	„	—	1
Maps, Plans, Awards, &c., ...	„	—	1
Presentment (Contract) Books, . . .	1833-65	3	—
Presentments	1575	—	1
Proclamations, ...	„	—	1
Voters' Register, ...	„	1	—

72. Purchases from Sir Thomas Phillips' Library.

Records.	Catalogue Reference.	Date.	Vols.	Preta.
Dublin City:—Letters, Papers, Reports, and Chief Justice Cox's Judgment in relation to the election of Lord Mayor and Sheriffs, 1711-12, .	135	1711-14	1	—
Envoy at Foreign Courts:—Letters in connection with Mr. R. Southwell as Envoy, 1669-70 and 1680; and other Papers of 1664-65. Letters, &c., of Edward Southwell 1703-39 and 1704-10, including Account of Parliamentary Session, 1715, .	136/3 & 134/6	1664-1739	2	—
Fee Book on Orders, Warrants, &c., issued from Chief Secretary's Office, .	134	1706-7	1	—
Forfeitures, Papers relating to, . . .	136/2	circa 1688	—	1
Inquisitions, post-mortem, Entry Book of, .	135	1597, 1616-37	1	—
Irish Rebellion:—Sir E. Hyde's Narrative and other Papers. Also Instructions to Lord Ossory in 1675, .	157/3	1641-81	—	1
Kinsale, Papers connected with; and various documents relating to the Southwells and Public Affairs:—				
Governor of the Fort, Papers of Robert Southwell, senior, .	157	1659-79	—	1
Election:—Letters to Ed. Southwell concerning the Borough Election in 1744, and other matters, .	134/6	1733-44	1	—
Riot on swearing in of John Banbury as Sovereign, Papers concerning the, .	136/6	1672-3	1	—
Southwell Papers, private and public:—Correspondence and Papers of Robt. Southwell as to lease of Dromderrig in Kinsale property, .	1-5/7	1667	1	—
Letters to Ed. Southwell from Cork, Kinsale, &c., .	136/1	1650, 1702-4	1	—

Sir Thomas Phillips' Library—*continued*.

Records.	Catalogue References.	Date.	Vols.	Prob.
Kinsale, Papers connected with; and various documents relating to the Southwells and Public Affairs:—				
Letters to Ed. Southwell in 1701-3, 1714, 1722, and 1725, relating to Huguenots, Kilkenny, Lighthouses, &c.,	125/2	1701-25	1	—
Letters to Ed. and Sir R. Southwell, 1681, 1690, and 1702-6, relating to French Prisoners, Privateers, &c.,	125/3	1681-1706	1	—
Letters, R. Southwell, Senr., 1665-6, and Sir R. Southwell, 1690-3,	125/4	1665-93	1	—
Presbyterians and other Dissenters, Papers relative to,	126	1708-12	1	—
Public Affairs, Civil, Military, and Parliamentary:—				
Civil :—				
Letters and Papers of Robt. and Edward Southwell relating to conversion of Roman Catholics; King William's quarters in 1690; R. Southwell, Senr., and Prince Rupert; and Treasonable Verses,	141/5	1690-1729	1	—
Letters from the Earl of Rochester, Lord Treasurer, to Ormond, on Irish Affairs,	152	1684-6	1	—
Letters on the Settlement of Irish Affairs,	157	c. 1690-5	—	1
" " Public Affairs,	151/2	1690-1725	—	1
" relating to Treasonable Verses, &c.,	141/9	1690-1725	1	—
Letters concerning Parliamentary Proceedings, death of Lord Capel while Chief Governor, appointment of Lords Justices, &c.,	132/1	1696-7	1	—
Letters to England from Lord Capell, Lord Deputy, and the Lords Justices,	154	1694-6	1	—
Letters and Papers, 1722-24, Advice to Ormond, 1703, with a List of Chief Governors, 1690-1703, King James' Officers taken as Anglican Bishops, &c.,	141/2 & 5	1703-24	3	—
Letters of Ed. Southwell,	141/4	1723-26	1	—
Letters and Papers connected with the Government of Ireland, Lord Abercorn and dukedom of Chatelherault, &c.,	141/1	1718-27	1	—
Military :—				
Proposals for regulating the Military Establishment and Defence of Ireland by the Earl of Dartmouth,	121	1683	—	1
Letters from Earl Rochester, Lord Lieutenant of Ireland, &c., to Wm. Blathwayte, Secretary for War, relative to Military Matters,	152	1704-6	—	1
Letters from Secretary Downes, &c., to Ormond, Sir Robt. and Edward Southwell, mainly on Military Matters,	152/1	1704-29	1	—
Parliamentary :—				
Letters from A. Saunders, M.P. for Taghmon, to Ed. Southwell, London, relative to Parliamentary Proceedings in connection with Lord Chancellor Cox, &c.,	153	1715	—	1

SIR THOMAS PHILLIPS' LIBRARY—*continued.*

Records.	Catalogue Reference.	Date.	Vols.	Prds.
Parliamentary :—				
Letters of Capt. R. Stewart to Rt. Hon. E. Southwell, Secretary of State, relating to Proceedings in Irish Parliament, Wood's Patent, &c.,	163	1723-114 & 1726	—	1
Revenue, Pamphlets relating to, with Instructions to Justices for regulating Cities,	162/1	1682-83	—	1
Sarsfield's Estate at Lucan, Letters of Sir Theophilus Jones, Sir R. Southwell and others, relative to claim of farmes to,	160	1684-5	—	1
William III. :—				
Addresses from Counties to King William (original) ; Papers connected with Popish Plot and Robt. Southwell's supposed complicity, Petitions, &c.,	124	1678-99	1	—
Letters from Sir R. Southwell to Earl of Nottingham, written from King William's Camp during campaign of 1690, giving details of the Battle of the Boyne, King James' Flight, Siege of Limerick, &c.,	142	16))	1	—

73. Presented by Rev. Dr. Groves, Monkstown, co. Dublin.

Records.	Date.	Vols.	Prds.
Chancery Affidavits (Miscellaneous),	1745-1846	—	1
„ Petitions,	1688-1761	—	1

74. From J. H. Samuels, Esq., Registrar, diocese of Dublin.

Records.	Date.	Vols.	Prds.
Dublin Diocese Marriage Licence Grant Books,	1672-1695	1	—
„ „ „	1712-1741	5	—

75. The Deeds affecting the right of the Crown, deposited here by the Quit Rent Office during the year, number fifty-three ; of these forty-six are Conveyances of Crown and Quit Rents.

Sorting and Arrangement of Records.

76. The re-arrangement of the Chancery Answers has been completed from 1569-1771, containing 10,966 fasciculi made up

into 1846 brown paper parcels. This completes the series of Chancery Bills and Answers, and experience has shown the change to be very advantageous to the quick handling of the Records and their preservation from damp, dust, and decay. The same process has been commenced for the Equity Exchequer Bills and Answers, and has advanced from 1787–1850 for the latter, and from 1790–1850 for the former. comprising together 8,574 fasciculi made into 1245 brown paper parcels.

77. One thousand one hundred and sixty-three parcels of Records from the Clerks of the Crown and Peace of the counties of Carlow, Cavan, Derry, Down, Kerry, Louth, Meath, and Sligo, and one hundred and sixty-seven parcels of Census returns 1841 of the City of Dublin have been stamped, in addition to those stamped from day to day before being submitted to public inspection.

78. Six parcels of the Parochial Returns of the Dioceses of Raphoe and Tuam, eighty-nine of Parliamentary Petitions, and sixteen of Parliamentary Returns have been numbered with type.

79. One hundred and nine parcels of See Leases of the Dioceses of Aghadoe, Ardagh, Kilmore, Limerick, Ossory, Raphoe, and Tuam; twenty-four parcels of Building Papers of Armagh, Raphoe, Tuam and Waterford, and forty-three parcels of Patents, Titles, Visitations, &c., of Ardfert, Cashel and Emly, Down and Connor, Ferns, Leighlin and Ossory have been folded to a uniform size.

80. The Cause Papers of the Court of Chancery were arranged in dictionary order in four classes under the names of the four last surviving or retiring Masters, viz:—Murphy, Litton, Brooke, and Fitzgibbon, or the Receiving Master, which arrangement was found in practice to be confusing and unfair to the public, as it often happened that the Cause sought for had been in more than one Master's office. It has, therefore, been deemed advisable to throw the four collections into one, and, at the same time, as it was found that they were deteriorating from exposure on the shelves and from being folded in four and tied together in parcels, the opportunity was taken of flattening them, as had been done with other Cause Papers, and arranging them in brown paper parcels. This process has been advanced as far as the end of letter E, making 8855 bundles of Cause Papers.

81. Two thousand five hundred and eleven Marriage Licence Bonds of the Diocese of Cork and Ross, and twelve hundred and eighty-two of the Diocese of Cloyne, have been repaired, sized, and pasted on guards; one Parish Register of ninety pages, sized and re-bound; one hundred and twenty volumes of Records, and one hundred and twenty-six volumes of Patents of Invention bound.

Indexing and Calendaring.

82. The draft Index to the Grants and Wills of the Diocese of Dublin, 1800–1858, has been engrossed, and is ready for printing, and will be published as Appendix III. to this Report.

83. Indexes have been completed to the Ardfert Grant Book, 1827-1801; the Armagh Marriage Licence Books, 1826 1832, 1832-1837, and 1837 to 1845; the Ferns Will and Grant Book, 1823-1882; the Ossory and Leighlin Marriage Licence Book, 1822-1882, and the Meath Grant and Marriage Licence Book, 1822-1857.

84. Indexes have been completed to the Marriage Licence Bonds of the Diocese of Armagh, 1727-1845 (3 volumes); Clonfert, 1789-1844; Down, Connor, and Dromore, 1721-1845, and Limerick, 1727-1844.

85. An Index has been prepared to the 26th, 27th, 28th, 29th, and 30th Reports of the Deputy Keeper, and printed as Appendix II.

Proceedings under the Parochial Records Acts, 38 & 39 Vict., c. 59, and 39 & 40 Vict., c. 58.

86. The Annual Reports of Parochial Officers having custody of Records under Retention Orders were all duly received.

87. The Retention Orders which had been issued up to the commencement of the present year number 571.

88. A Register of the parish of Furgney was repaired and rebound at the request of the parochial custodian.

89. The Records of the following parishes which became attachable during the year 1897 have been removed to this Department.

Parish.	County.	Vols.	Baptisms.	Marriages.	Burials.
Ballymascanlan,	Louth,	8	1801-1897	1803-1846	1817-1897 (a).
Creagh,	Cork,	1	1803-1897	1813-1845	1813-1896
Eglish,	King's,	1	1834-1895	1834-1846	1834-1897
Inishkenny,	Cork,	3	1809-1897	1808-1844	1818-1894
Moytew,	Longford,	1	1831-1890	1841-1849	1871-1895
Rossmire,	Waterford,	1	1834-1890	1833-1849	1833-1897

(a) Also two burial entries, 1801 and 1806.

90. In the following parishes the Records which became attachable were allowed to remain in local custody under Retention Orders.

Desertmartin.
Clanmavis.
Killala.

Portadown.
Tullow (Diocese of Leighlin).

91. A Parish Register of Owenduff, containing entries of baptisms and burials from 1828 to 1845 and of marriages from 1828 to 1868, which was reported missing in 1891 (see 23rd Report, page 17, and 25th Report, page 86) has been recovered, and was retained here for rebinding.

92. Two Registers of the parish of Carrigrohane containing entries 1787-1801 and 1824-1847, which were not returned upon

the original Inventory, were recovered by Rev. F. Dobbin, Chancellor of Cork Cathedral, the Incumbent of the parish, and deposited here under a Warrant of the Master of the Rolls.

93. The former of these two books is earlier in date than the three volumes which have been of record here since 1877, and the latter fills up a gap in the series of entries contained in those three books. The years covered by the various entries for this parish now are :—

Baptisms,	.	.	.	.	.	.	1712-1871
Marriages,	.	.	.	.	.	.	1787-1844
Burials, .	.	.	.	.	.	.	1789-1871

94. In the case of the parish of Moydow a Register, containing entries of baptisms, marriages, and burials from 1794 to 1810 would appear to have disappeared between the date of the return of the original Inventory in 1875, and the time when the Register became attachable in 1897.

95. Upon the application of Rev. Canon Walsh, D.D., the Order of the Master of the Rolls respecting the records of the parish of St. Peter's, Dublin, was supplemented by an Order allowing the baptismal register of St. Stephen's, Dublin, 1866-1868, to remain in the custody of the Incumbent of the last-mentioned church, its place of deposit being still within the parish of St. Peter's. At the request of the respective Incumbents of the parishes of Clonsast and Maryborough permission was given to change the position of the safes provided for the Records of those parishes, and new Retention Orders were granted, when the work had been done, in the usual course.

96. The fees received in stamps during the year amounted to £869 2s. 6d., being a decrease of £15 15s. 6d. on the amount credited in 1896.

TABLE OF FEES, 1897

Month.	Inspec- tions.	Traces of Maps.	Attend- ances.	Folios at 1s.	Folios at 6d.	Amount.
January, . .	248	—	—	185	5,180	73 1 9
February, . .	282	1	—	169	3,036	75 4 0
March, . . .	264	1	—	254	2,878	109 9 0
April, . . .	191	8	—	417	1,660	73 8 8
May, . . .	230	1	6	469	1,897	79 14 0
June, . . .	208	2	—	114	2,602	67 3 0
July, . . .	258	—	—	275	2,191	76 7 4
August, . . .	188	—	—	118	1,763	50 17 9
September, . .	169	—	—	145	1,056	43 1 6
October, . .	542	3	—	130	1,633	59 10 6
November, . .	289	2	—	75	2,834	74 7 6
December, . .	163	8	1	250	1,766	79 19 6
Total. . .	2,877	18	2	2,576	22,513	863 9 6

In addition to the above, fees on copies made for Public Departments have been remitted to the amount of £28 8s. 6d.

97. I have to acknowledge the following donations :—Two volumes of Record Publications by the Keeper of the Records of Scotland ; a volume entitled " The Winders of Larton," by the author, F. A. Winder, esq. ; and the second volume of the " Hand-list of Proclamations," by the editor, the Right Honorable the Earl of Crawford.

98. A considerable number of searches have been made during the past year in connection with matters of historical and antiquarian interest. Among the subjects investigated I may mention the History of the parishes of Antrim, Ardee, Fermoy, Monkstown, Tullylish, and Whitechurch ; the Dublin Hospitals ; the Irish Regiments of Guards ; and the 14th Hussars (formerly 14th Regiment of Dragoons).

Dated at the Public Record Office,
   Four Courts, Dublin, this Four-
   teenth day of May, 1898.

J. J. DIGGES LA TOUCHE,

*Deputy Keeper of the Public Records and Keeper
of State Papers in Ireland.*

I humbly certify to your Excellency that this Report is made by the Deputy Keeper of the Public Records and Keeper of the State Papers in Ireland, under my direction, pursuant to the Statute.

A. M. PORTER,

Master of the Rolls.

APPENDIX I.

Mr. H. F. Berry's Report on the MSS. purchased at the sale of
Sir Thomas Phillipps' Library.

These MSS. are chiefly connected with the Southwell family,
and formed part of the collection originally put up for sale in
1834 by Thorpe, of Bedford-street, when a large number of the Southwell papers were acquired for the British Museum. The twenty lots
comprise thirty-six separate items, namely, two entry books of correspondence, and one of inquisitions *post mortem*; twenty-seven volumes of
bound letters, &c., and six portfolios of unbound letters. One of the
entry books was already indexed; the other volume and the calendar
of Inquisitions have now been fully indexed, and a catalogue of all
the remaining documents has been prepared.

The inquisitions entered in the volume referred to range between the
years 1610 and 1633, with one of the year 1587, and as proving the
importance of its acquisition, a list of no less than seventy inquisitions
recorded in it, which are not to be found in the Record Commissioners'
printed catalogues, has been compiled (See p. 59.) The book, which
is entitled "Liber omnium inquisitionum transcriptorum in Officio
Rememoratoris Thesaurarii et Secundi Rememoratoris scaccarii ex
curia cancellariæ Hiberniæ" is noted as having belonged to the library
of Sir James Ware (who had been Auditor General), and also as having
formed an item in the Chandos collection.

The index to it has been prepared in the names of the parties on
whose decease the inquisitions were taken, arranged by counties, on a
plan similar to that adopted by the Record Commissioners.

The Kildare and Inchiquin families, the lords Dillon, the Roches,
Conways, and many other ancient houses are represented in this volume.

Next in order of date, (save some of the papers connected with the
Southwell family) is a MS. account of what passed in the wars and
rebellion of Ireland from 1641 to about 1653—a short view and
condition of the Kingdom of Ireland—written by Sir Edward Hyde
(afterwards Earl of Clarendon) when at Cologne, which may be taken
as the foundation of his printed history.

There is also an account of the costs incurred in subduing the Irish
rebellion of 1641, and the damage sustained by the Protestants. Other
important documents are the Account of Sir Adam Loftus, Vice-
treasurer, of the Revenue of Ireland, 1638-9-40, and the manuscript
Instructions by the Commissioners of the Commonwealth of England, to
be observed by the judges and officers of every court of justice, held
weekly in any city or town in Ireland. (This last has a note to the
effect that it was printed at Dublin by William Bladen, 1659.)

A very interesting paper is the Report, dated from London, 23rd
November, 1658, drawn up by W. Dickinson for Robert Southwell,
Junior (afterwards Sir Robert Southwell), on draining and reclaiming
the bogs in Ireland.

Among these manuscripts, there are papers and correspondence
connected with three generations of the Southwell family. Commencing
with Robert Southwell, customer of Kinsale, who amassed a large
fortune and died in 1676/7, we next meet with his distinguished son,
Sir Robert, born in 1635. He was clerk of the privy council, and
envoy extraordinary to several foreign courts, subsequently becoming

principal Secretary of State for Ireland. Sir Robert accompanied King William on his campaign in 1690, his letters from the various camps being of extreme interest. He held office until his death in 1702, when his son, Edward Southwell, succeeded him as Chief Secretary. Edward Southwell married firstly, Lady Elizabeth Cromwell (afterwards Baroness Cromwell), daughter of Vere, Earl of Ardglass, the "Lady Betty" so frequently mentioned in the correspondence; and secondly, Anne, daughter of William Blathwayte, Secretary of State, &c., to William the Third, through which alliance, the papers of the last named came to be united with the Southwell MSS.

The earliest parcel contains depositions, petitions and memoranda, 1635–1640, in the matter of certain charges made by Robert May, of Dublin, against Robert Southwell, the elder, of neglecting his duties as customer and collector of the Port of Kinsale, of non-observance of rules and regulations, and specially for having made money out of some Virginia tobacco imported in 1636 by Captain Batson and John Slowly. In March and April, 1637–8, Southwell was detained in confinement in Dublin in the house of a Mr. Haughton and of one Gunnis, a pursuivant, whence there are letters to his wife and to Sir Phillip Percivall, whose son, Sir John, afterwards married Southwell's daughter, Katherine.

One of the papers is endorsed "1649 articles of Tristram Whitcomb, against Mr. Southwell, for his loyalty to ye King and assisting Prince Rupert (taken to London, 1698)," but no such document is in the parcel. In 1648 Southwell, out of his own resources, provisioned and supplied with money some ships under command of Prince Rupert at Kinsale, without which timely assistance the Prince could not have put to sea, and there is a copy of a King's letter, dated 28th September, 1660, for a grant to him of certain lands in county Cork, forfeited by Philip Barry oge and James Mellifont, as satisfaction for his advance.

As a large portion of the Southwell estates lay in the neighbourhood of Kinsale, its interests and concerns, as well as those of individuals among its townsfolk, are frequently dealt with in the collection. Kinsale harbour was celebrated for affording shelter to the home and foreign navies, as well as ships laden with merchandise from every part of the globe, and in the 17th century, a naval station with dockyard, was established there. During the Irish wars, and especially at a time when smuggling and privateering prevailed to such an alarming extent on the South and West coasts, this harbour, from its position, because of great importance to the trade of the channel, and hence, a good deal of the correspondence is taken up with it. Among the papers are rent rolls and surveys of Kinsale and its liberties, in 1658. The corporation proposed to become tenants of certain of the forfeited lands, but Southwell's interests appeared to conflict with theirs, and there are memoranda in his handwriting, detailing services rendered by him in the concerns of that body. A remarkable memorial exists, asking for an assistant minister, and praying that Taxax (Tisaxon) and Rincurran parishes should be united to Kinsale, which states that many of the popish inhabitants had joined with the English in securing the town against the Irish.

Vol. 1½ is occupied with the unseemly riot and quarrel that took place on the swearing in of John Sexbury as Sovereign of Kinsale, in 1672. Sir R. Southwell was himself present, and addressed a letter to the lord chancellor on the subject. When the case came before the council he was examined, and an order was made attaching Cookin, Stowell, and other rioters.

In October, 1690, Banfield (Southwell's steward) gave him an account of some prizes in Kinsale harbour, which he said were there when the forts were taken, and which Lord Marlborough claimed as his right. During 1691-2, the Danish auxiliary forces were quartered in Kinsale, before being shipped for Flanders, and the soldiers committed great waste and injury, especially in Southwell's woods, and they cut down orchards, and digged up gardens for some distance round. A French regiment was also quartered on the town, and fifty horses of Colonel Churchill's regiment grazed on Sir Robert's lands at Rincurran for over a year.   There is a list which was sent to Southwell, received 27th March, 1691, and endorsed by him—"Great men lodged at my house at Kinsale"—which includes the names of the Earl of Marlborough and Brigadier Churchill.   In 1703 Colonel Oglethorpe wrote that there was then in Kinsale, on board the "Swede"—a prize, as good wine as in France, which might be got for His Grace (Ormond). The French prisoners in Kinsale in 1705 caused a considerable amount of anxiety and trouble ; there was no proper prison, and their ill health, consequent on confinement and overcrowding, became a serious source of danger to the townspeople. Lacroix, writing on 1st June, 1705, reports that the prisoners were recovering ; he had sent them to Brown's mill under a guard, to wash and take the air while the prison was being cleaned and perfumed with burnt tar, and clean straw laid in it. He hoped soon to have a prison and hospital built. James Maule made a remarkable statement, namely, that the ministers and elders of the French Church in Cork had asked him to speak to the French prisoners of war, (born protestants), with a view to learning if they would be willing to serve on board Her Majesty's ships, getting a bounty, but the officers in charge would not allow him to meddle with them. Three young fellows, protestants, however, came to him, declaring their willingness to serve the Queen and never return to France.

In 1703, there is news of those on board a privateer being very civil to the inhabitants of the Isles of Arran, the crew paying good rates for everything they took. "In the old Duke of Ormonde's time, a garrison was kept in the Isles, which greatly secured the shipping on the coast."

Throughout the correspondence, there are frequent glimpses of the war on the Continent. Thus, in March, 1691, Southwell writes that his son (Edward) got back from Flanders to the Hague, and His Majesty had gone to the army to try and raise the siege of Mons. A letter from Cork, dated 23rd January, 1704, conveys the intelligence that a ship which left Gibraltar twelve days before had put into Kinsale, with news that the place held out stoutly, and only two small frigates there. Alderman Hoare, of Cork, who communicated this intelligence, had some days before made proposals for victualling Gibraltar from Ireland.

In May, 1705, a packet boat from Lisbon put in at Dingle, which brought a full account of an attack on Valenza, Estremadura, by our forces under Colonel Duncanson, the Dutch and Portuguese. "Nothing can be attempted this summer campaign as the enemy outnumber us in cavalry." A list is given of killed and wounded from the regiments of Lord Portmore, Blood, Brudenell, Duncanson, and Cunningham. In June, 1705, there was news from Cork of the fleet destined for Portugal having sailed with 2,500 men on board. Intelligence also arrived of a fleet of large ships (about 100 sail), supposed to be the Dutch, that sailed from Portsmouth in May, having been seen standing in for Lisbon.

Some of the papers are specially concerned with Sir Robert Southwell's suspected complicity in the Popish plot. There are depositions before a committee of the House, list of Oates's papers, informations of various persons as to the plot, and orders to search documents left by the Spanish Ambassador in Humphry Weld's garden; also an order of the Lords for attendance in March, 1678, of Sir John Nicholas, Sir Robert Southwell, Sir Philip Lloyd, and Sir Thomas Dolman with papers relating to the plot, together with a vindication of Southwell by the House of Lords, and votes of the Commons.

That portion of Sir Robert's career in which he acted as Envoy to foreign States is also represented in the collection. In 1670, he wrote vindicating himself from some censure on him in the Court of Lisbon, asserting that Verjeux (de Verjus) was the slanderer. The Conde de Miranda, Ambassador at Madrid, had honoured him in every way, and in Paris he had visited de Macedo, the Prince of Tuscany, and others, all zealous for the honour of Portugal, who treated him with every respect.

In 1680, Sir Robert was envoy to the court of Frederick William, Elector of Brandenburg, and there is some correspondence between them in Latin, with translations into French. One letter deals with the seizure of the vessel "Charles the Second," near Ostend, and in another from Berlin, Southwell gives Secretary Jenkins an account of a long audience with the Elector. Tangiers (Queen Catherine's portion) is also mentioned, and a correspondent in Lisbon gives Southwell the points reserved by the British Commissioners for a conference with reference to it in 1683.

The variety of subjects dealt with in these papers is only limited by the number of questions daily and hourly being brought before men like Southwell, holding responsible executive positions. The Chief Secretary for Ireland in the 17th and 18th centuries was in constant communication with the Military, Naval, and Revenue authorities; he gave all instructions as to transports, embarkations, and war vessels convoying merchantmen, and was instantly informed of the movements of privateers in the Channel. The defences and fortifications of the country and the guarding of the coast were his constant care, so that in addition to his parliamentary duties, he was responsible for several departments, which have since those days been withdrawn from such oversight, and placed under separate officials, responsible for their management. During a period when the religious question in Ireland was of such a burning nature, the conduct of enactments against the Roman Catholics must be added, and a number of documents in the collection are conversant with the established Church, its clergy, convocation, the popery laws, foreign priests and friars coming into the kingdom, as well as with the presbyterians and other dissenters. Several of the documents bear also on the French Huguenot churches, and their pastors, and on the French pensioners.

Many letters and reports affect the city of Dublin, its streets and institutions; municipal affairs take up a large space, and the questions involved in the deliberate opposition shown to the Government by the Town Council in 1712, in the selection of Mayor and Sheriffs, are amply discussed, much fresh light being thrown on these events.

The disposal of the forfeited estates in Ireland, the Court of Claims, and the carrying out of the enactments consequent on the articles of Limerick and Galway, afforded Southwell much anxiety, and the question of the revenue resulting from the forfeitures is frequently dealt with.

The volume entitled "Irish Book" (which contains Mr. Secretary Gwyn's book plate), is an entry book of letters written by the Earl of

Rochester, lord treasurer of England, and his secretaries, to the lord lieutenant and lords justices of Ireland, the Commissioners of the Revenue, and many others on various questions that came before the King, from February, 1684, to December, 1686. The correspondence is chiefly conversant with revenue matters, fines, custodiams, quit rents, customs, and army clothing and accoutrements.

Lord Rochester subsequently became lord lieutenant of Ireland, and one portion of the miscellaneous correspondence consists of letters on military matters written by him between July, 1701, and July, 1702.

The next volume is the original entry book of letters written by Lord Capell, when lord lieutenant, and the lords justices from February, 1694–5, to May, 1696, most of them addressed to the Duke of Shrewsbury, and it contains the book plate of Algernon, Earl of Essex, 1701. One letter, dated 9th July, 1695, gives the first hint of the State Paper Office, Lord Capell recommending its establishment in the Castle, for deposit of the books of entry of Chief Governors' orders, and be is "content to begin with his own books, and have them the first of record." In another letter, Dr. Ashe, bishop of Cloyne, is reported to be desirous of the rank of privy councillor, which is "interpreted as a desire in him to be excused from residing on his bishopric; he is a young deserving gentleman, but this his early ambition gives great offence both to the clergy and the nobility here."

The Council always sent to England the Bills introduced, and the correspondence deals with the more important ones, such as those concerning the forfeited lands and the Roman Catholics. The King's prerogative in the matter of Money Bills is often mentioned.

Lord Capell made grievous complaint of Lord Chancellor Porter's high handed proceedings and haughty tone with regard to himself, and in some of his letters to the Duke of Shrewsbury will be found a narrative "of the passage" (as His Excellency terms it) that occurred between them. Capell wished to make William Neave, whom the Chancellor considered his personal enemy, a Serjeant-at-law, and the latter refused to seal the patent. The lord deputy exercised the utmost forbearance in the matter, but felt it right to lay before His Majesty certain cases in which Porter was shown to have avowed the Irish interest, and favoured adherents of King James. The cases were those of Shapland in Wexford and Mr. Knox (whose commission as Sheriff he had opposed the sealing of), and full reports of them are given. The matter ended in favour of Lord Capell's nominee, as a letter was addressed by him to the King on 15th January, 1695–6, thanking his Majesty for having ordered the Chancellor to seal Neave's patent.

In May, 1696, Capell became so ill, that he retired to Chapelizod for rest, and appointed Lord Blesinton, and Colonel Wolseley lords justices, and His Excellency's case becoming serious, they wrote urgently as to providing for the Government in case of his death, which occurred on 30th May, 1696. The Judges and Council had been consulted, and not being unanimous in opinion as to whether the Commission of the lords justices determined with his death, the latter decided on not acting without the King's special directions, though the law officers were of opinion it did not determine. Those opposed to the Lord Chancellor now said that he used every means to get himself appointed lord justice. In pursuance of the Act 33 Henry VIII., the Council was summoned, but with undue haste, and he was elected, to the chagrin of Lord Meath, who specially wrote to Shrewsbury that he had himself expected to be chosen. Lord Meath went the length of asserting that Porter had pretended a letter from England saying that the King wished his appointment. That it was a popular one is evident from the fact that there were bonfires and illuminations in his honour, but certain members of the house of Commons brought forward a complaint as to the methods adopted by Porter, the articles as to which were rejected. Certain of the Irish Peers, including lords Meath and Blesinton (the ex-lord justice), petitioned against the appointment, as of evil consequence to the kingdom, and a breach of the privileges of the peerage. The Speaker of the Commons put an affront on the Lord Chancellor the night the latter made his defence before that House, by causing the horses of his coach to be stopped, to allow his own to pass, which was taken as an indication of the very strong feeling against him.

In February, 1703, the Duke of Ormond was appointed Viceroy of Ireland. The lords justices gave minute directions for His Grace's reception on landing, and there is an account of Ormond's progress from London to Dublin between the 20th May and 4th June, 1703. There is a very important memorandum drawn up by Edward Southwell, principal Secretary of State, for Ormond's guidance in the government, in which he recommends to him the care of the Church, and his keeping a strict hand over the army, especially the recruiting department. The army here never to be of less strength than twelve regiments of foot, six of horse, and four of dragoons. In England's emergency during the late war, no project for money answered so well as the £14 per cent. Act; if one at £15 per cent. were calculated for Ireland, "all nations would send their money thither."

Southwell also dealt with the hardship of ships for Ireland being compelled to unload in England, pay the English customs duty, and then reload for Ireland, and he recommended that the English duty should be collected in Ireland. He hopes for encouragement of the linen manufacture, and the victualling of the Navy in beef and butter, largely from Ireland.

In March, Joshua Dawson, Secretary to the lord justices, wrote to Southwell that the opinion here was that the Duke had no power to sign commissions as lord lieutenant, until he had taken the oaths. The lords justices had received no order from the Queen as to obeying directions from His Grace, which they ought to have, such orders having been given in Lord Rochester's case; these orders were subsequently renewed for Ormond. A letter of 2nd March, 1702-3, debated the question of the lords justices' commission not being vacated by Rochester's surrender, and as to their holding directly from the Queen.

In Dawson's correspondence with Southwell at this time, there is a remarkable statement as to his views with regard to English methods in Irish revenue matters. He asks that a certain letter of credit should not charge the transport of some regiments for Holland to the Irish Revenue, "which cannot bear such an expense, but that same be paid out of the Treasury of England, which, if you don't take care in, they will most certainly place it upon us, as they always do, when they have an opportunity."

In the same connexion, it is interesting to note that with a view to the approaching coronation (Queen Anne's), new trumpets and kettle-drums were required for the "State," the serjeant-at-arms wanted a new mace, the late King's cipher was to be taken off the coats of the heralds and pursuivants, state canopies, &c., and the whole matter was to be laid before Ormond, who might get all in England, if he liked. Rochester had brought over new liveries and states, &c., but in his

D

case a letter had arrived, charging £1,500 for them, "the first of that sort that Ireland ever paid for" (adds Dawson).

Secretary Dawson's rather lengthy epistles supply much interesting information, and two or three of them written soon after Southwell's appointment as Chief Secretary, deal with the accommodation provided for him in the Castle. Over the offices were lodgings with reception rooms, bedrooms, &c., and there was ample stabling in the yard. Dawson informed his chief that sealing wax was always supplied from London—pretty good—and he begged him to purchase ten or twelve pounds of the best, and 2,000 or 3,000 Dutch quills, "which cannot be got in Ireland, and have to be sent for to London. We can have paper here of the best sorts, yet cannot always be provided with it; send a quantity to Alderman Allen to Chester, to be sent with other things."

Lot 153 consists of letters from Anderson Saunders (M.P. for the borough of Taghmon, county Wexford) to Edward Southwell, which give an account of affairs in Parliament and in the city, during December, 1713, and January, 1713-4, as well as of the proceedings against the lord chancellor, Sir Constantine Phipps. As a precaution, these letters were nearly always sent under cover to his wife's mother, who resided in London. The Government party was at this period involved in difficulties, and the power of the Whigs was growing.

In a letter to Ormond, Saunders mentions that the Lord Chancellor, the chief judges and others are all to be struck at, and he tells Southwell that Ormond himself "keeps much at Chapelizod, never concerning himself with what is done at Chichester House." In telling of the House having come to resolutions in favour of the city charters, he lays all at the Lord Chancellor's door, and asserts, from his knowledge of the temper of the House, that unless the whigs are gratified by his removal, no further supply will be voted. As to the alleged offer of £500 to get a good Common Council, Tucker and Gore, on their examination before the lords, fully cleared the Chancellor. "If the whigs are gratified they will not stop there, but will expect the country to be put into their hands; hopes for the joyful news of Her Majesty's recovery." "From the lukewarmness in a certain place, it is given out that the Tories have the Pretender in view. The leading men are for continuing their persecution of the lord Chancellor, &c., not thinking the Kingdom safe (as they say) from the Pretender until they have the care of it put into their own hands."

In addition to parliamentary questions already alluded to, there are several copies of Acts during the Session of 1695, and letters as to the voting in the House. During 1696-7, Parliament was engaged in considering measures for confirming the articles of Limerick and Galway, for settling a Militia, and as to the outlawries, the linen manufacture, the education of the Irish in the Protestant religion, &c., together with legislating on such matters as planting certain lands lying on Cork Harbour and the Shannon with Protestants. The Council in transmitting the bills to England made copious observations on them.

In a long letter addressed to the Earl of Nottingham, on 24th December, 1715, is given a full account of the late Session.

A memorial about the Tillage Bill in Ireland at this period contains the statement that in a foreign market, Irish corn will hardly yield half the price of English. The encouragement of this Bill will not prejudice English trade abroad, for where such is transported no Irish victual will sell at any price, except in cases of great scarcity.

The Irish Government of the day had to deal with a good deal of sedition and disrespect to the Queen and Ministry, and some of the cases have further light thrown on them by the papers here. There is a letter from an unknown person, to Lord Rochester, dated 3rd February, 1702-3, complaining of the Primate and the Bishop of Derry; at the table of the latter the health of the Princess Sophia is said to be the only toast. In January, 1711, a seditious letter addressed to Father Murphy, Cavan, was dropped at the Four Courts, and a copy of it is among the correspondence. In November, 1712, we have the examination of Richard Spann, of Dublin, as to language used by Rev. Mr. White, a Protestant divine, against the Queen and her Ministry.

A sensation seems to have been created in Dublin by the finding in Lloyd's Coffee House on Cork Hill on 27th November, 1712, of some treasonable and scurrilous verses entitled "Honest Resolves," a copy of which accompanies the depositions taken in the matter. Edward Lloyd, proprietor of the tavern, and some members of his family, were examined, and so serious a view did Government take of these verses, that on the case being laid before the Council, a proclamation was issued, offering £500 reward for the author of the verses and £300 for the publisher. (See list of Proclamations, No. 46-1714. Twenty-third Report, Deputy Keeper of the Records, page 58).

In June, 1713, Mary Lloyd gave information to her father, the said Edward Lloyd, that at three o'clock in the morning of the 23rd, six gentlemen appeared on the balcony of the Globe tavern, and drank whig toasts, which she, (unseen by them) heard and wrote down. Colonel Johnson, son of Baron Johnson, and one Buttel were two of the party.

Among the satirical pieces connected with the politics of the day is preserved in this collection a curious one entitled, "The Chequer, or one with t'other, a miscellany of old plays revived by a Medley of new poets" which is endorsed "Plays writ by members in Ireland, by Mr. Crow." From a large number of titles of such plays, the following are selected to give some idea of their character, each no doubt referring to some well known incident or scandal of the period.

The Dean's duel, or a soldier for the ladies, by Brig——r Cun——ham, dedicated to Lord Shel——n.

Le Malade Imaginaire, by Sir Thomas So——all.

The Modish husband, by Sir Stand. Har——ge.

Sir Timothy Treat-all, acted at the Queen's Arms Tavern, Fleet Street, by Mr. Al—n Brod——ck.

As bearing on matters intimately connected with the prosperity of the country, and the cares and duties of the Government of the day, there will be found among the papers, correspondence and reports on such subjects as the supposed introduction of the plague into Kerry. In January 1710/1 letters arrived from Baltimore announcing that it was reported there that a Dantzic vessel had brought the plague to Kerry, and the lords Justices at once caused communications to be addressed to Mr. James Julian, the High Sheriff, and Maurice FitzGerald, the Knight of Kerry, directing them to take active steps to prevent the spread of the sickness. They also sent a long detailed report of their proceedings to Ormond.

About the same time, the Council directed Captain Thomas Burgh, surveyor general, to report on the anchorage at Dalkey Island, with a view to its being used as Quarantine quarters for ships coming from plague-stricken places. Captain Burgh reported that it was unfit for such a purpose, as no ship could lie there with safety, and the sum of

£4,311 4s., was his estimate for the construction of a secure harbour and pier. Certain persons were also appointed by the Lord Mayor of Dublin to report on the establishment of a harbour at Dalkey and the report bears date February 1711/2. In November 1702 Sir Thomas Southwell had reported as to the harbours on the west coast of Ireland.

In November, 1706, there is a report of the Commissioners of the Revenue on the light houses round the coast, which deals with those at Howth, Hook Tower, Kinsale, and Isle Magee.

Lord Abercorn wrote to the authorities from Strabane in September 1714, stating that the Light House patent which had been granted to Sir Robert Reading, (who had had a salary of £500 for having expended £2,600 in the erection of 6 light houses) now formed part of his marriage settlement, he having married a daughter of Sir Robert and his wife, the Countess of Mountrath. Lord Abercorn begged that he be allowed to surrender the patent, owing to his inability to perform the requirements of the House of Commons, by reason of the heavy charges in building additional light houses and the expense of maintaining lights in them. The petitioner in this case was James, 6th Earl of Abercorn, and though unconnected with public affairs, it may be of interest to notice here that in the collection are copies of letters written by him in January and February 1712/3 to his wife, his son Lord Paisley, and Lord Anglesey, relative to the family claim to the dukedom of Chatelherault in France, which enter fully into the case and furnish many details.

There is a curious report in French on the planting of timber, and the state of the country districts is frequently referred to. In December, 1728, we find that the three preceding harvests had been bad, so much so that a subscription list was opened for the supply of imported corn for the use of the poor in the North, which was largely contributed to.

A document of much interest, written from Kinsale in 1695, gives Southwell the current rates of commodities, which are stated to be subject to constant fluctuations in that part of Ireland, according as the coast is secured from privateers, or not.

Some light is also thrown on the payment of rent. Thus in December, 1704, William Taylor, who had been passing accounts in Chancery connected with Sir John Percivall's estate in county Cork, writes that he cannot see how the tenants can discharge their rents in that part of the kingdom, owing to the "general calamities of the time." At a later period, in July 1735, Edward Brinn, writing from Kinsale, says that the rents of Scilly cannot be got in, the poverty of the people being so great; there is such scarcity of provisions, that he has been obliged to send them money and other necessaries for their fishing craft.

Lot 134 is a volume almost entirely conversant with the proceedings of the Town Council of Dublin in the later years of Queen Anne's reign, which occupied so large a share of public attention. An attempt was made to establish the right of the lord Mayor for the time being to nominate three candidates and to compel the Aldermen to elect one of them as his successor; similarly as to the Sheriffs. This led to a protracted contest between the Aldermen of the city on the one side and the Lord Lieutenant and Council, acting on the powers of approval and disapproval given them by the new Rules, on the other. The lords justices wrote on 3rd of May 1713 that Alderman Barlow, who had been disapproved of before by the Government, had been again elected lord Mayor, and their Secretary, Dawson, wrote later on that the example of Dublin had had an evil effect on other corporations, instancing particularly that of Coleraine.

The lords justices expressed much satisfaction on being informed that Her Majesty permitted them to express disapproval of the Mayor and Sheriffs elected; matters were then amicably arranged, for there is a draft of an Address to Ormond from the lord Mayor in September, 1712, apologizing for the recent conduct of the Town Council, and rejoicing that good relations had been re-established between the City and the Government. It is marked, "given 30th September to Lord Donegall," and "1st October, Archbishop brought this paper from yᵉ Recorder." There is a "brief of the City case," in Sir Richard Cox's autograph, which commences, "Faction is the root of it, and 'tis a branch of the silly division amongst Irish Protestants into Whig and Tory." Accompanying these papers is a list of the Common Council of the City of Dublin, by their Guilds, annotated with regard to the conduct of each member on the recent occasion. Thus, "red letters stand for staunch churchmen; black for Wh—g or P——terian, black part and red part for those that have trimmed."

One of the most important papers in this volume is Chief Justice Cox's judgment (in his own handwriting), dated 30th April, 1714, on the case of the Sheriffs of Dublin, which holds that the office of Sheriff is not void at the end of the year, and that the Sheriffs are bound to act until their successors are sworn in.

Bartholomew Van Homrigh when lord Mayor in 1697 petitioned for a collar of SS in lieu of the mayoral one taken to France by Terence Dermott, and there is a copy of a King's letter for payment to him of 500 guineas, to procure a collar, which was to have a medal with the King's effigy attached to it.

In 1712, new buildings were required to be erected in the castle for the Treasury and other offices, such as those of the Auditor General, Commissary General, Registrar of Deeds, Barrack Board, &c., and Captain Burgh, surveyor general, reported against a site that had been proposed in the back yard of the castle, inasmuch as the only way to these offices would be through Castle-lane, a narrow passage; the buildings also would be too near the "ramps" leading into the upper yard, which would then become a public thoroughfare. Secretary Dawson wrote to Southwell, giving reasons for adopting one (of what he considered) two more suitable sites; 1. the place where the old Council Chamber stood, as the new one is to be within the Castle. 2. part of the yard attached to Lucas's coffee house, which adjoins the Castle wall, to which a passage might be made from the new way into the Castle: Lord Cork's Commissioners might be induced to sell. Southwell on behalf of the Government, made a proposal to purchase for £1,200, Lord Burlington's interest in the Barbadoes or Tom's Coffee House, &c., in Castle-street. This stood at the Castle Gate, on the right hand side turning into the Castle, and was finally demolished by the Commissioners for widening the streets leading to the Castle. In April, 1712, there had been proposals from Lord Cork's creditors as to this site, and in November of that year, John Rathborne was treating with Government for compensation for some houses on Cork Hill, through which a passage was to be opened to the Castle. The business in his case was long delayed, for as late as January, 1723, the Duke of Grafton recommended Rathborne's case and payment to him, in compensation for houses knocked down in making a proper passage from the Blind Quay to the Castle.

A document dated 10th May, 1728, was drawn up by Thomas Burgh, Surveyor General of Works, as to building a Parliament House. The Commissioners of the Revenue, who appear to have made representations on the same subject some time before to Lord Rochester, in April, 1703, wrote further on the pressing necessity for a new Custom House, the old one being ready to fall.

Dublin bar received its share of attention, for in December, 1721, the House of Commons passed a resolution in favour of Captain John Perry's proposals for increasing the depth of water over it, and making a basin for ships to lie in. With regard to the convenience of travellers between the city and Ringsend (most of whom would be on their way to or from England), the establishment of a proper service of cars between Ringsend and Lazy Hill (the present Townsend-street) was under consideration.

In 1712, the Trustees of the Hospital to be founded under Dr. Stevens' will petitioned the Government for a piece of ground in the Phœnix Park, held from the Crown by Thomas Proby, which he was willing to resign.

On the 3rd July, 1701, General Erle, in writing to Southwell, from Dublin, took occasion to relate how " this town has been transported in expressing their zeal for his Majesty upon the ceremony of erecting the King's statue a horseback, which was performed [on the anniversary of] the day he fought the battle of the Boyne."

The collection under notice contains a number of papers and documents connected with the various forms of Religion, whether of the Established Church, the Roman Catholic, the Dissenting bodies, or that professed by the French Huguenots, who formed, what afterwards became, flourishing colonies in Ireland, and whose ministers and their flocks were the especial care of the Irish Government. With regard to the Established Church, in addition to the necessary correspondence as to vacant bishoprics, unions of parishes, appointments of clergy to Crown livings, &c., we learn that a bill for translating the see and cathedral of Tuam to Galway was transmitted by the Irish Council to England; this was stated to have originated in the Commons house, and was drafted in the " hope of making Galway a protestant town, and so, a great security to that part of Connaught." There is also some correspondence as to convocation, in 1703, when Ormond was addressed on the subject of provincial writs. The original address of the clergy of the Church in the province of Ulster to King William the Third in 1600 is preserved, and it contains a large number of autograph signatures.

There is a very remarkable memorandum on the Union with Scotland, as it might affect Ireland, the latter portion of which deals with episcopacy, but the earlier part may be quoted here as well. It suggests that England and Scotland will probably unite in keeping Ireland poor. England totally destroyed our woollen trade, so it is to be feared she and Scotland will destroy our linen trade in favour of the latter, or rather, England will encourage the linen trade in Scotland, to prevent the Scotch falling too much into the woollen trade. The Union is desirable, and England may turn the balance at any time, if she take Ireland into the scale, for we should send Members to both houses, staunch to episcopacy and the English interest. " Episcopacy is so interwoven with our laws and constitution, so agreeable to Monarchy and so gentlemanlike a Government in the Church that we are fond of it." The writer adds that the English protestants in Ireland, who chiefly make up our representatives, are immediately descended from England.

In 1703, the Archbishop of Dublin was in correspondence with Secretary Southwell, on the question of the Dean and Chapter of Christ Church being exempt from visitation.

After the war, it was found necessary to have a special chaplain (or curate) to minister to the spiritual wants of Charlemont Garrison; the Rev. John Dunlop, who was appointed, was refused maintenance by the rector of the parish, and the matter was referred to Lord Charlemont, who reported that the Garrison had great need of an additional clergyman.

In 1711, the heads of the Established Church became very active in taking steps for the conversion of the Irish people professing the Roman Catholic faith, and schemes were drafted and reasons offered for incorporating a Society, by means of which they were to have sent amongst them Established Church ministers skilled in the Irish language, to read the Scriptures and preach to them in their own tongue. There is a draft of a royal letter (without date) on the state of the papists in Ireland.

A copy of King James's Latin letter to the Pope "written with the King's own hand" from Dublin in 1689, together with a copy of a national letter to that Monarch, against the British, "mended by ye Popish bishop of Clogher," 1688, exist, and there is also a copy of the Indulgence granted by Pope Alexander VIII, found in July, 1690, in the pocket of a rebel killed in Ireland.

One of the lots (135) is a volume of letters and papers relating to the Dissenters. Hugh Rainey of Magherafelt, by his will, proved in 1708, made provision for the education of 24 boys as Presbyterians, and an Act of Parliament was to be promoted, to confirm the will, &c.; a note in Southwell's handwriting specifies that a clause should be inserted, to prevent their being brought up in principles prejudicial to the Established Church.

In 1708, Narcissus, Archbishop of Dublin, petitioned, that no support out of the grant of £1,200 per annum from King William to the Presbyterian ministers, be allowed to the dissenting teacher established in Drogheda, who was drawing people away from their allegiance to the Church, and the Grand Jury of Drogheda made a presentment against the Northern Presbytery for setting up a conventicle there. From about the last mentioned period to the end of Queen Anne's reign, the presbyteries seemed to have become active in asserting themselves, and their boldness gave Government and the Established Church some trouble. A printed "Call to prayer—a serious call from the city to the country," (a copy of which is among the papers) was largely circulated among their members in 1712, and may have had the effect of stirring them up to fresh efforts in furthering their views and tenets. The Grand Jury of Cavan presented against a Synod that met at Belturbet, and the Dean of Kilmore and others wrote full accounts to the Castle, asking that steps be taken against such in the interests of the Established Church. On this the Presbyterian ministers of the North addressed Ormond, the lords justices, and even the Queen herself, against any further "persecutions intended against the congregation at Belturbet."

In August, 1713, Mr. Westenra Waring, High Sheriff of the County Down, forwarded to the Castle a letter from Captain Brent Spencer, dated from Lisburn in 1713, stating that on his learning that a certain Mr. M'Cracken intended to preach there again, he sent two constables, but the doors were locked and M'Cracken would have been rescued on any attempt to arrest him. He added that a company of foot might be ordered out for the purpose from Belfast. Government would not order

M'Cracken's prosecution, but the justices at Belfast declared their intention of undertaking it.

As bearing on the Huguenot refugees, a letter was written by the Castle authorities to the Duke of Shrewsbury in January, 1695, enclosing an address of the Commons and a memorial of Baron de Virazell, chief agent of the French protestants here.   There is also a long document in French, which is undated, containing Dean Abbadie's proposals for a French colony.   Jacques Abbadie was chaplain to the Duke of Schomberg, and there is a petition from him, written in his native language, praying for employment.

On the arrival of Ormond as lord lieutenant in 1703, the French colony addressed him, and there are preserved the "Harangue" of congratulation offered on their behalf by Pastor Barbier, and portions of a sermon preached before His Grace, by Monsieur Lenzac, both in French.

As in the case of many other bodies, dissensions began to rise among the members of the Huguenot congregations scattered through the country.   Pastor David wrote a long account (in French) to Ormond of an unseemly occurrence that took place in the congregation at Kilkenny in June, 1705, through M. Renoult's desire of being sole French minister there.   In 1713, Jourdan wrote also to Ormond, detailing an unhappy division that had occurred in the French Church at Waterford.

Perhaps the most interesting volume in the series is that which contains rough copies and drafts of letters from Sir Robert Southwell to Lord Nottingham, written during the eventful days of June, July, and August, 1690.   It would seem as if Macaulay were unaware of this collection of contemporary letters, dealing with a period of so much importance in his great work ; while careful to enumerate all his authorities, he makes no mention of Sir Robert Southwell's correspondence.   One of the letters dated 9th June, written from Chester, gives an account of King William's journey from the time of his leaving Kensington on 4th.   Southwell accompanied the King all through the campaign as principal Secretary of State, and in Volume "4" is a coloured plan of the King's quarters, as laid out in each place, showing the names of the ministers in attendance, the suite, &c., with the positions assigned each : Southwell's quarters are next those of the King himself.

The party embarked on board the " Cleveland " yacht at Hoylake on 11th June, and reaching Carrickfergus, they sailed up to Belfast. There are letters from camp at Loughbrickland, Dundalk, and Drogheda, and that from the latter, dated 1st July, gives a full account of the slight wound received the day before by King William, when reconnoitring ; "at this instant comes news to my tent, that Count Schomberg got over some of the upper fords (of the Boyne) and defeated some squadrons of the enemy's horse."   The King ordered his tents to be taken down, and having won the decisive victory of the Boyne, he is found encamped next day at Duleek, from which place Southwell again wrote, describing the battle and narrating the deaths of Duke Schomberg and Dr. Walker ; in his letter he mentions that the King had directed the Duke of Portland to draw up an account of the battle.   On 4th July, the army was near Swords, and from the camp there, Southwell gives an account of King James's flight, as the story had reached his party ; he adds " I suppose Duke Schomberg's body will be deposited in y° Chief Church in Dublin, till there be opportunity of some solemn interment."

The letter from camp at Finglas is of much interest and gives a still fuller account of the flight of the defeated King. "Duke Tirconnell lost much in camp, since I have in my hands his entry book of private letters, &c." "This day being Sunday (6th July), His Majesty rode in great splendor to the cathedral, where all services of the Church were solemnly performed. The bishop of Meath and the bishop of Limerick were there, and Dr. King, an excellent man and a great sufferer, preached much to the purpose. The old Mayor and Aldermen did the honors of the City . . . . As our King, who looked and appeared this day better than ever I saw him, returned by the Castle, he rode in to see the place, but did not alight."

The camp was next pitched at Crumlin, from which place the King moved on 11th by Castlewarden to Inchiquire, close to Ballitore, county Kildare, and on 14th, writing from that place, Southwell gives a full account of the King's proceedings in Dublin, in restoring the magistrates, seeing the clergy, appointing Commissioners as to the rebels' property, pricking Sheriffs, &c. The next letters are from Wells, Bennetsbridge, and Carrick, from which place, Southwell writes on 24th July that Waterford had surrendered on the same terms as Drogheda. On the 27th the King left the camp at Carrick, and went back to Chapelizod, intending to pass over into England, but on 29th Southwell states that he had changed his mind and resolved to turn back to the army again, his idea being that once he assured a passage over the Shannon, he might then return home; Sir Cloudesley Shovel was to be ordered to hasten to Plymouth with the larger vessels of the fleet under his command and the smaller were to remain in the river at Waterford till further order. There is a letter of 4th August from camp at Goldenbridge, and several written from the King's camp at Limerick during the siege, which was raised on 30th August. As descriptions by an eye-witness, these last are important, minutely detailing, as they do, all the circumstances of the siege. In one, Southwell speaks of their men being preserved in the trenches "by an invention of woolbags, which are planted like palissadoes before those who work, and are musket proof. These are made by one Mozsters, a Dutchman, who is comptroller of our artillery, an excellent artist, and were never made use of before unless a little at the siege of Bonn." "Having written thus far at 6 of y° clock (22nd August) we heard a great shout from the Hill, and the meaning is that the Tower is already fallen down."

On 25th, there is an account of bombs, and hot bullets being thrown into the town, which set fire to houses, hay, &c, taking many hours to quench. "His Majesty did very unwillingly consent to this expedient, but most of the officers were urgent for it, as the only way to expedite the work." The previous day, Southwell wrote that when the King rode out to observe the city on its supposed weak side, and only Count Schomberg and another with him, the Count's horse was shot by a musket bullet.

"I have wrote by His Majesty's orders to Sir Cloudsly Shovell, that if he should happen to find at his coming to the Shannon, a squadron of the French that were much superior to him, he should forbear to make any rash attempt."

"By the post that went this day, your lordship had all that relates

E

to the misfortune that befel our Artillery," a disaster fully described in
a letter of 13th August. It happened at Cullen, within ten miles of
the camp, when Sarsfield at the head of 500 horse and 60 dragoons
fell suddenly on a small convoy, conveying eight pieces of artillery,
small bridge boats, tools, &c. The guard consisted of about 80 troopers
and 12 Switzers.

After these exciting scenes and camp life with the army, Southwell
turned his attention to the settlement of the kingdom, beginning with
the judges and law officers. Pine, Ryves, Cox, Temple, Rochfort,
Keating, Echlin, and Hartstonge are among the names of those suggested
for places. In a memorandum of 30th September, 1690, he notices
that there is a great defect in arms and ammunition in the kingdom.
As to the oath to be imposed on those that will remain inhabitants of
Dublin, he has doubts of its being seasonable, it being of the highest
importance to His Majesty that the Irish be reclaimed and gently
drawn to submit to his authority.

During the next year, events of the utmost moment in the history
of the country were being transacted, and this collection throws further
light on the conduct of some of the actors in this very real historical
drama. Mr. Justice Cox in his capacity as Governor of the county
Cork, showed an amount of activity that would have done credit to an
experienced military commander, while at the same time he exercised
the functions of a Judge of Assize for Munster. There is a letter from
him to Southwell, dated 8th October, 1691, in which he says that
Athlone having been taken and Aughrim won, and with Galway and
Limerick in our hands, the war is at an end, "and if matters are well
managed, there can never be an Irish rebellion in this Kingdom any
more." He then proceeds to give an account of his government in
Cork; "as for the enemy, having, as I believe, killed and hanged not
less than 3,000, whilst I staid in the County of Cork, and taken from
them, in cattle and plunder at least to the value of £12,000" he says
that he felt himself in a position to divide £360 among Colonel
Townsend's troop, after which Colonel Beecher and the Western gentlemen got a prey of £3,000. He claimed to have brought the Militia up
to 36 troops in 6 regiments, and 26 companies in 3 regiments, and to
have kept a frontier, 80 miles long, from Tullow to Sherkin, and all did
not cost county Cork above £1,200.

The general correspondence included in this collection extends to the
year 1744, but the letters from about 1715 to that year are com-
paratively few in number.

Reference to the catalogue of all the documents which has been
prepared, will afford a means of obtaining information on many other
subjects of interest not touched on in this report.

INQUISITIONS, NOT IN RECORD COMMISSIONERS' CATALOGUE,
INCLUDED IN ENTRY BOOK OF INQUISITIONS (Lot 436
Phillipps' MSS.).   *Vide ante* pp. 37 and 44.

Name.	Date.
Cork County.	
Theobald Roch, . .	3rd October, 1610.
Thady mcDermody Carty, . .	13th August, 1623.
Donogh oge McCartye, .	12th January, 1624.
John Stmaurice Roch,	10th September, 1624.
Donnell O'Cahall, .	5th April, 1627.
Cork City.	
Philip Gould, .	25th October, 1618.
William Meade,	4th August, 1671.
Down County.	
Gerald, earl of Kildare, .	5th April, 1623.
Dublin County.	
Henry Burnell, . . .	20th January, 1617.
Morrogh, lord Inchiquin, . .	12th April, 1610.
John Browne, . . .	5th January, 1620.
John Fitzsimons, . . .	5th January, 1620.
Dublin City.	
Robert Piphoe, . . .	18th February, 1653.
Kerry County.	
Jenkin Conway, . . .	9th April, 1622.
Kildare County.	
John Allen, . . .	30th March, 1625.

Name.	Date.

Kilkenny County.

Thomas Comerford, . .	. 6th July, 1618.
Gerrald Grace,	. 6th July, 1618.
Walter Walsh,	. 6th October, 1619.

Kilkenny City.

Robert Roth, . .	. 18th April, 1622.

King's County.

Oliver, Lord Lambart, . .	. 23rd October, 1618.

Limerick County.

Sir Edward Walsh, knight, .	. 1st April, 1620.
Nicholas Stritch, .	. 4th January, 1621.
John Bourke, . .	. 14th January, 1621.
John FitzHubert Bourke,	. 14th January, 1621.
Walter Bourke,	. 14th January, 1621.
David O'Heany,	. 14th January, 1621.
Richard Wale,	. 14th January, 1621.
Ownic O'Heine, .	. 15th January, 1621.
Oliver Stephenson, .	. 27th August, 1621.
Francis Trenchard, .	. 9th January, 1622.
Richard oge Bourke, .	. 18th October, 1622.
Maurice Baskely, .	. 9th January, 1623.
Garrett Harbret,	. 12th March, 1623.
Donal O'Brien,	. 16th April, 1623.
John Southwell, .	. 16th April, 1623.
James Gould, .	. 23rd August, 1623.
Edmund Wolfe, .	. 5th September, 1623.
Edmund Purcell, . .	. 30th March, 1624.
William Ryan, . .	. 30th March, 1624.
Thomas FitzGerald alias Cam,	. 3rd August, 1624.

Names	Date.

Limerick County—continued.

David Bourke, ...	30th August, 1624.
Nicholas Creagh, ...	30th August, 1624.
Gerald FitzGerald, ...	30th August, 1624.
Richard oge Whyte, ...	30th August, 1624.
Gerrald mcWilliam mcShane Annacior, . .	24th September, 1624.
Cornelius Haly, ...	24th September, 1624.
Tindy O'Heyne, ...	24th September, 1624.
William mcHenry O'Mullegan, . . .	8th October, 1624.
Thomas FitzGerald, ...	8th October, 1625.
Edward Lay, ...	12th March, 1627.
Mortertagh McBrien, ...	27th August, [ ].

(Louth) Drogheda.

John Fottrell and John Congrave, trustees of Sir Ambrose Forth, knight.	23rd July, 1618.

Mayo County.

Ballyioghdolla and Ardnevy, .	25th September, 1618.

Meath County.

John Bath, ...	21st April, 1587.
Gerald, earl of Kildare, . .	17th August, 1691.
Christopher Bath, . . .	18th October, 1624.
Richard Balfe, . . .	9th January, 1628.

Roscommon County.

John Muriche, ...	19th July, 1621.
Theobald, lord Dillon, . . .	19th September, 1628.

Tipperary County.

Nicholas Walsh, ...	21st April, 1622.
Nicholas Whyte, ...	1st April, 1623.
Richard Keatinge, ...	10th April, 1623.
Godfrey Prendergast, . . .	10th April, 1623.

Name.	Date.
Waterford County.	
Patrick fitz Thomas Whyte, .	29th April, 1622.
John Browne,	14th September, 1625.
John Wise,	14th September, 1625.
Wexford County.	
John Sutton,	18th January, 1817.
Richard Synnott,	1st October, 1818.
James Synnott,	2nd October, 1818.
Nicholas Roch,	1st January, 1822.

APPENDIX II.

INDEX TO DEPUTY KEEPER'S REPORTS.

(TWENTY-SIXTH TO THIRTIETH, BOTH INCLUSIVE).

(References are by Roman Numeral to Report and Arabic Cipher to page).

INDEX TO DEPUTY KEEPER'S REPORTS XXVI.-XXX.—*continued.*

INDEX TO DEPUTY KEEPER'S REPORTS XXVI.-XXX.—*continued.*

DUBLIN: Printed for Her Majesty's Stationery Office,
By ALEX. THOM & CO. (Limited), 87, 88, & 89, Abbey-street,
The Queen's Printing Office.